"Retreat!" John Koenig yelled. "Back off, all of you!"

Koenig waved his arms and, gesturing, turned to face the crater.

And then he saw i̶

And froze.

It was a creatur̶ ̶̶̶̶̶̶e—blurred and fiery, rising ̶̶̶̶ ̶̶̶ ̶̶̶̶e center of the huge crater. Space dust rose and fell from its flailing appendages, the starlight gleaming from something that looked like polished marble, ebony mixed with pearl.

And from above, the Eagle came diving down, laser flaring a beam of light so intense that Koenig, blinded, stumbled and fell. He could remember with horror the picture of the last thing he saw: a small figure swept from its feet, lifted, spacesuit and all, and hurled into the crater's angry mouth.

John Koenig waited for the end!

ALIEN SEED
was originally published by
Futura Publications Limited.

Books in the Space: 1999 Series

Published by POCKET BOOKS

ALIEN SEED

E. C. TUBB

PUBLISHED BY POCKET BOOKS NEW YORK

ALIEN SEED

Futura Publications edition published 1976

POCKET BOOK edition published June, 1976

L

This POCKET BOOK edition includes every word contained
in the original edition. It is printed from brand-new plates
made from completely reset, clear, easy-to-read type.
POCKET BOOK edtions are published by
POCKET BOOKS,
a division of Simon & Schuster, Inc.,
A GULF+WESTERN COMPANY
630 Fifth Avenue,
New York, N.Y. 10020.
Trademarks registered in the United States
and other countries.

ISBN: 0-671-80520-7.

Printed in the U.S.A.

To my Mother—
a unique woman

CHAPTER ONE

Koenig heard the sound as soon as he stepped into the cavern and halted, eyes searching the dimly lit interior, finally locating the source among the cluster of men and women assembled at the centre of the open expanse. Bergman was among them and he turned, smiling, as Koenig reached his side.

"A nice touch, don't you think, John?" He gestured to the object of their attention. "Somehow it belongs."

Koenig looked at a fountain.

Someone with more than a touch of imagination had built a thing of beauty, setting it in a bowl of polished stone edged with concealed lights that threw a kaleidoscope of gentle luminescence on the arching fronds of transparent leaves. Entranced, he watched the interplay of colour, the water spouting high from the nozzles—an artificial rain that rose to curve to fall in musical cadences.

"Do you like it, Commander?" Nancy Coleman, the botanist in charge of Rural Area One, was justifiably proud of the installation. "Do you approve?"

Koenig nodded and looked at the walls of the man-made cavern in which they stood. They rose to merge in a common point high above the floor of the chamber that had been gouged from the Lunar rock. The floor was levelled, paths running between wide beds of loam; soil made of crushed stone with humus added, chemicals and minerals incorporated with other ingredients to fashion a familiar dirt.

In it, one day, would grow flowers, blooms serving no purpose other than to please the eye and nostrils. There would be grass on which lovers could stroll and games could be played. Bushes and even trees grown from precious seeds. A miniature forest set far beneath the Lunar surface, an oasis to which they could come to remind themselves of what they had lost.

Earth itself, their home, taken from them when the tremendous explosion of accumulated radioactive waste had blasted the Moon from its orbit and sent it on its incredible journey.

A black day in September 1999.

One he would never forget.

"John?" Bergman was watching him. "Do you want to give the order?"

As the commander of Moonbase Alpha it was his right, but a commander could have too many rights and it would be wise not to insist on those that held no real importance. Others must be made to feel as if they shared authority, as they certainly did share responsibility.

"John?"

Bergman was impatient to see the culmination of his project, eager, perhaps, for praise—he was human enough for that.

Koenig said, "A moment, Victor. Nancy, who designed the fountain?"

"Constance Boswell. Connie?"

She was young, lovely, her smoothly rounded face holding an elfin beauty. An electro-technician attached to Coleman's staff. Koenig smiled at her as she came close to a halt, standing before him. Taking the commlock from his belt, he activated it, spoke to the face that appeared on the screen, then held the instrument out to the girl.

"Here, Connie. You do it."

"Commander?" Her eyes glanced upwards to the shadowed apex of the cavern. "You mean—"

"I want you to give the order, Connie," he said. "You've earned the right. The rest of us just dug out this place, but you've beautified it with your fountain. So go ahead."

For a moment she hesitated, a little smile quirking a corner of her mouth and then, quickly, she said, "Let there be light!"

Above a sun blazed into being; not a real sun, but something so near as to give that impression. A mass of lights radiating a carefully selected section of the electro-magnetic spectrum that closely matched that of Earth's sun. Koenig felt the warmth of it, knew that if he stayed long in its radiance he would acquire a tan.

To the commlock the girl said, "Complete cycle."

The light faded a little, then more, then died to create a simulation of twilight, of dusk, of final night. Koenig heard the inhalation of those watching as lights began to wink from the roof of the cavern, artificial stars set in a familiar pattern.

And then the dawn, a milky opalescence strengthening to a roseate glow, the brilliance of early sunrise.

"Wonderful!" A woman drew in her breath. "I never thought . . . Victor, thank you!"

"There should be bird-song," said Connie as she handed Koenig back his commlock. "I could arrange it, light-triggered recordings and strategically placed speakers. Simulacrea, too, artificial birds set in artificial trees. We could place one there, and another just there, and two over by the far opening."

She was talking more to herself than to him, and Koenig knew it. Taking the commlock, he watched as she moved away to halt at the side of a young man, her face animated, both laughing, both moving off with arms interwound.

"Connie has a point," said Nancy. "And I'd like to do something with those walls. Some of the men suggested we fashion them into a likeness of the interior of a cathedral. One mentioned Chartres. Did you ever see it, Commander?"

"Once."

"I never had the chance," she said regretfully. "And now I never will. I've seen slides, of course, and even a hologram, but nothing can convey the impression of antiquity and size, the dedication of those people who gave their labour for the love of God. Could we—?"

"Within limits, Nancy, yes." Koenig softened his warning with a smile. "But you can't use essential materials, power or labour. Yet if people want to use their recreation time working to decorate this place, I won't object. However, don't forget why we built it in the first place."

Not for fun, nor for show, but as a place in which to grow food. An addition to the hydroponic tanks and yeast vats which, together with the algae tanks, provided the Base with sustenance. The cavern would serve a double purpose and later, with luck, could be turned into a park and garden.

"I won't forget," she promised. "And you won't regret this, Commander. I—" She broke off as his commlock hummed.

Paul Morrow was on the screen. He said, without preamble, "Commander, you'd better come at once to Main Mission."

Dr Helena Russell picked up a card, looked at it for a moment, then placed it face down on the desk before her.

"Star." The girl lying supine on the bed was thirty feet away across the ward in Medical Centre. There was no possible way she could have seen the design. "You want me to continue, Doctor?"

"Please, Lynne, if you're not feeling too tired."

"Tired?" Lynne Saffery gave a chuckle. "How could I get tired just lying here?"

And yet there was strain as Helena had warned when, after her series of tests on the personnel had determined their extrasensory perception potential, Lynne had been asked to volunteer for further investigation. Now she was beginning to get a little bored.

"Star," she said as Helena looked at more cards. "Circle, circle, square, cross, wavy line, star, wavy line, cross, cross, square, circle, star, star . . ."

A complete run of a hundred, each of five cards studied twenty times in random order. Anyone, by naming only one design, could achieve a success rate of twenty percent. Lynne had scored seventy-eight.

Helena pondered the figures as she made a notation on a sheet clipped to a board. One high score could be due to chance, two due to coincidence, but for more there had to be a reason. On a score of tests Lynne had gained results far in excess of the statistical average, a finding enhanced by other tests, many made without her awareness.

"Once more, Lynne, if you please."

"Must we, Doctor?"

"Getting tired?"

"Bored, rather." The girl stretched then, smiling, said, "Well, why not? Anything to help the cause."

Helena picked up the cards, shuffled them and, holding them face down, slipped the top card from the pack and laid it, still face down, on the desk.

"Lynne?"

"Star," said the girl after a moment's hesitation.

Helena made a notation, then placed another card face down on the first one.

"Circle," said the girl after a moment. She sounded unsure. "At least I think it is."

"Please do your best to concentrate. And this?"

The girl's voice gained firmness as the run progressed. At the end she said, "How did I make out?"

Badly, but Helena didn't say so. Again she pondered her findings. The girl made high scores only when Helena looked at the cards, low when she did not—a fact which tended to eliminate clairvoyance and precognition; neither should be affected by the human intervention.

The girl smiled as Helena approached the bed, then looked warily at the machine as she pulled it towards the head of the cot.

"More tests, Doctor?"

"A few simple ones, if you have no objection. I want to take readings of your brain wave pattern on the encephalogram while you are under mild sedation. It is important to the success of the experiment that you be wholly relaxed. Have I your agreement?"

"Why not?" Lynne shrugged. "Go ahead, Doctor, a good sleep never hurt anyone yet."

Within moments it was done, the girl lying at rest, her eyes closed, her breathing shallow. Quickly Helena attached the adhesive electrodes to various points on the skull. As she reached towards the controls of the machine, her commlock sounded the attention signal.

It was Koenig. He said, "Helena, we're on Yellow Alert. Have Medical stand by."

"John!" She stared at the screen, at the face with its peak of dark hair, the eyes that had seen too much, the mouth that betrayed the inner sensitivity. "Is something wrong?"

"As yet we can't be sure. I'm just warning you before the general alarm. Have you any emergencies?"

Helena glanced at the girl. Asleep she was no problem, and it was better to leave her that way than to jar her metabolism with the shock of conflicting drugs. But there were others, some due for surgery, none, fortunately, in a critical situation.

"No, John. No emergencies." And then she added, because she was both a woman and human and therefore curious, "What is it? What's happening?"

"Probably nothing, but we can't afford to take chances. There's something in space heading our way. We don't know what it is and, until we do, we stand ready for anything."

"For how long?"

"Until it hits us, passes us, or we wipe it from the sky."

"John! Do you—"

But he was gone, the connection broken, the tiny screen blank. And, as much as she wanted to be with him, her place was in the Centre, which she controlled.

From where she stood before her instruments, Sandra Benes said, "No response, Commander. As far as I can determine, it is just a lifeless mass of rock. No answer has been received to the entire range of signals we have transmitted and there is no discernable radiation emitted from the located object."

"Kano?"

"Computer agrees, Commander. All findings to date are consistent with the mass being a scrap of stellar debris."

Rock blasted from the world to which it had once belonged to drift through space as the asteroids drifted around the Sun between Mars and Jupiter. A lonely wanderer as was the Moon itself.

Leaning back in his chair, Koenig looked at the direct vision ports. Beyond lay the empty immensity of the void, the stars that shone with a remote indifference, distant suns with their own orbiting worlds. Each was a possible haven for those who, trapped in the Moonbase when the explosion had occurred, had been left with no choice but to fashion a new life on the bleak and barren satellite.

His eyes lowered to study the Lunar surface, the ground pocked with craters, seamed with fissures, the hollows thick with a dust as fine as powdered talc. Airless, waterless, those essential ingredients of life having to be reclaimed from the Lunar stone; liquids and gases torn from their chemical prisons to be used, recycled, used again and again.

A closed ecology in which only power was plentiful, the atomic generators breeding their own fuel.

"Commander?" Morrow spoke without turning in the big chair facing the main console. "Your orders?"

Decisions, rather; always it was a matter of decisions and, always, Koenig was acutely aware of the danger that, at any time, he could make the wrong ones. A slip, a miscalculation, and the life that maintained a precarious hold on the razor-edge of survival could be pushed that little bit too far. Strained beyond the capability of available resources or faced with a threat it could not handle, Moonbase Alpha would become the tomb of hundreds riding a dead world.

Koenig glanced at the main screens. As yet the object was too small for even the high magnification to resolve, its presence known by electronic sensors. The lack of response to signals told against it being a vessel, but that was not conclusive. It could be a potential enemy playing dead, or something so alien as not to use the same means of communication as the Alphans. Or, as Kano had said, it could be nothing more than harmless rock.

Harmless—as long as it didn't come too close.

A hope that David Kano negated as he checked the computer read-out.

"Bad news, Commander. Computer plots the course as being on an intercept path with Alpha." His dark face was sombre. "The estimated area of impact is within three miles."

Koenig said sharply, "Potential damage?"

"A direct hit would totally destroy the Moonbase. Even if it hit at the edge of the predicted area, the impact would produce internal stresses and the shock wave would result in extensive damage."

Morrow said, "Red Alert, Commander?"

"Not yet." They still had time. "I want to see what that thing looks like. Have Alan take an Eagle and make a close scan." He added grimly, "An armed Eagle. Full destructive and defensive equipment. Passive observation unless the Eagle is attacked or I order otherwise."

As Morrow leaned over his console, Koenig rose and stretched and glanced around Main Mission. Like a well-oiled machine, it had met the emergency, each at their position, the Moonbase on full defensive standby. A good team, he thought, one trained by previous emergencies, knowing just what to do and how to do it. Crossing to a bank of screens, he studied the portrayed interior of the Moonbase. The Yellow Alert was in full operation; certain areas had been sealed and were guarded by purple-sleeved security men and other precautions had been taken, but its purpose was to instill an awareness of potential danger rather than an immediate hazard.

The touch of a button and he looked into Medical Centre. Helena, he noticed, was at her station and he watched the softly gleaming gold of her hair, the play of light and shadow over the strong contours of her face. A face with prominent cheekbones, wide-spaced eyes, a generous mouth and a determined chin. One which, at times, could be a mask.

"Helena!" He saw her turn towards the communication post and said quickly, "Just a routine check. There's nothing to worry about."

"At times, John, you are a master of understatement."

"Not this time—that I promise."

A lie, and he wondered why he had said it, wondered, too, why he had felt it necessary to talk to her. It would have been enough simply to scan, but he had a reluctance to spy, to watch without her knowing she was under observation. An invasion of privacy, and yet in the confines of the base it was almost impossible to avoid it. And, when the common security was threatened, there could be no time for minor considerations.

Another button and he looked into the newly opened cavern. Bergman, he knew, had arranged a small party to celebrate the occasion; a matter of small cakes and weak wine, the spirit more important than the actual food and drinks. He stood now in the centre of the throng, a glass in one hand, a cake in the other, his face flushed with pleasure.

An old face, seamed, the hair receding from the

domed skull, the ears tight against the bone. His eyebrows were bushy and the figure beneath his uniform was not as it had been. Taut muscle had yielded to soft contours and the firm skin had become crepey; yet, though his body had weakened, there was nothing wrong with his mind. Professor Victor Bergman was a genius who had chosen to live, study and work on the Moon. An honoured guest who had become involved with all the rest; one who had proved his worth a hundred times in the new and frightening circumstances in which they had found themselves.

One with a mechanical heart.

At times he joked about it, resting his hand on his chest where surgeons had implanted the tiny electrical pump that had replaced the natural organ. A miracle of science that had enabled him to live when earlier men would have died. A side effect had been the detachment it had given him, a mind ensured of a regular supply of oxygenated blood, one unaffected by the emotional disturbances of the natural organ. Some hinted that it was a disadvantage, that he lacked human warmth and understanding, his appraisals of any situation too coldly precise and devoid of any trace of human compassion. Koenig didn't hold that opinion and had little patience with any who did. To him Victor Bergman had a greater depth of humanitarian understanding than most. A dedicated scientist who had earned every prize and award he'd been given and one worthy of the highest respect.

Now he was enjoying himself beneath the sun he had created, at home in the tiny paradise he had planned and helped to build.

"Eagle One approaching target area, Commander," said Morrow from his console. "Shall I put it on the main screen?"

"Yes." Koenig knew the value of participation and every man and woman in Main Mission would be curious. "Alan?"

Carter was on the screen. His face, behind the open face-plate of his helmet, was bewildered. He said, "I'm within visual range, Commander, but you're not going to believe this."

"Why not?"

"I . . . well, see for yourself."

His image vanished; another took its place. The vista of space, distant stars, the luminosity of the void, shimmering patches of remote galaxies, the whole awe-inspiring immensity of the universe.

A backdrop to what lay in the foreground. A something which was . . . incredible.

CHAPTER TWO

It was relatively small, the body slightly larger than a pair of Eagles, a thing of intricate facets and oddly set planes, dappled with abstract markings that seemed to shift and turn even as they watched, to adopt new and more disturbing configurations. A mass of rock, perhaps, one that had suffered a series of impacts that had formed and shaped the surface as wind and rain could fashion stone into oddly familiar likenesses. Glass, fused and cooled and rendered opaque with conflicting stresses, patches shearing, planes yielding, normal lines of cleavage distorted by alien forces. A sculptor's dream—a nightmare.

A mystery.

Koenig studied it, feeling his eyes slip from point to point as if they were fingers trying to hold and examine droplets of mercury. And, if the body was hard enough to accept, the mantle surrounding it was worse.

Not a mantle—more like wings. Not wings as are found on a bird, but sails. Yet not exactly like sails, but as tremendous filigrees of delicate lace. Yet not really like lace, but more like a—

"A web," said Bergman slowly. He had come to Main Mission in response to Koenig's summons. "Not a normal web, but those used by small spiders that use the wind to move them from place to place. They spin clouds of gossamer and use them like sails."

"Sails? In space?"

"Light has pressure, John," reminded Bergman. "It can be used as a wind."

"But not by that thing." Koenig was positive. "The area is too small and the mass too large. Light pressure alone would never move it. Right, David?"

Kano was busy at his station. "Correct, Commander. Computer says that it would be physically impossible for that object to be moved by the normal pressure of light." Pausing he added, "We have more accurate information on the course. The object will make impact within two miles of Alpha."

"No doubt?"

"None. Two miles is maximum."

And far too close. Again Koenig examined the odd thing they had found. The image, relayed from the attendant Eagle, moved as Carter made a circuit of the object. The body remained an enigma, the delicate-looking lace-like fabrication surrounding it, the same.

"How long to impact?"

"Twenty-one minutes, five seconds, Commander. We should be in direct visual contact within three minutes."

"Sandra?"

"Still no response to our transmissions, Commander. Negative on detected radiation emission. Negative on thermal differential. It's as dead as before."

Dead, maybe, but even so, a menace. A missile aimed at the heart of the Moonbase and which would bring total destruction with it. If it hit, they—all of them—would be dead. A decision to be made and Koenig knew what it had to be.

He said, "Paul, order three more Eagles to lift and take up position in a line from us to that object. One halfway out from the present positions, the others one third. All to be armed with a full compliment of nuclear missiles. Also alert the ground defences to stand by their launchers. Red Alert!"

Bergman said quietly, "John, you can't destroy it."

"Why not? Because it has an intriguing appearance?" Koenig echoed his impatience. "You know I've no choice, Victor. There's nothing else to do. Either we get rid of that thing, or it will get rid of us. You will pardon me for wanting to survive."

"But—"

"Alan! Prime your armament."

Incredulous, the pilot said, "You want me to blast it, Commander?"

"You've an alternative?"

"No, but—" Carter broke off, then said, his voice resigned, "You're the boss, Commander, but that thing looks so unusual, so strange. I can't believe that it's natural."

"And if it isn't, John, just think of what we could find inside." Bergman spoke with a quick intensity. "It could be a ship, one with a dead crew or one sent out on automatic control. Something could have gone wrong. It must be drifting, powerless, harmless aside from its course. It could teach us things we've never even imagined. A chance, John! How can we refuse to take it?"

From the computer Kano said, "Eighteen minutes to impact, Commander."

"There's your answer, Victor," said Koenig acidly. "That thing is heading straight into our laps. It may not want to, but it is about to kill us. I'm sorry, but we've no time for either discussion or investigation. Alan!"

"Commander?"

"Adopt a position for offensive action. Nuclear missiles. I want that thing volatised. Aim—"

"Wait!" Bergman gestured with the slide rule he had taken from a desk. "Give me a couple of minutes, John. Please."

"Sandra?"

"All readings still negative, Commander. The object is now on visual scan." She nodded towards a screen where the mysterious thing could be seen by direct magnification. The view relayed from Carter's Eagle was better.

Bergman said, "Give me some figures—the mass, velocity, total external area. Quickly, please!" He pursed his lips as he made notations, his fingers deft as he manipulated the rule.

As he worked Koenig said, "Paul, order Alan to fire a low-powered burst from his laser. Have him aim towards one end of that object. If there's life inside they might respond." He added, "And tell him to be careful."

He blinked as light flared from the screens, one bright with a view as seen from the Eagle, the other a wink of brilliance almost ˉlost against the stars.

"Eagles Two to Four heading for their positions, Commander," reported Morrow.

Koenig nodded. "Any signs of life, Sandra?"

"All readings negative."

From the screen Carter said, "Shall I try again, Commander? A heavy burst this time?"

"No. Adopt position for missile attack. David?"

"Twelve minutes," said Kano.

"Necessary force to volatise?"

"That won't be necessary," said Bergman. He smiled as he dropped the slide rule on the desk and waved the paper on which he had made his computations. "We don't have to destroy the object at all, John. Right?"

Koenig frowned. "What else can we do?"

"Divert it." Bergman glanced at the screens. "We can fire a missile so that the force of its discharge will

throw that object off course far enough for it to miss
the area of the Moonbase by a safe margin. Will you
give me permission to try?" Then, as Koenig hesitated, he urged, "Think of what we could find, John.
The Moonbase will be safe, and we have nothing to
lose but everything to gain."

Koenig was not a barbarian. He took no pleasure
in destroying for the sake of destruction, and his
curiosity had been aroused by the fantastic appearance of the object. If it was a lifeless lump of debris,
diverting it would save nuclear missiles. If it was an
artifact, as Bergman seemed convinced it was, then,
as he said, the gain could be tremendous. A gamble
worth taking, yet even so, he hesitated, conscious of
a nagging doubt. An elementary caution stemming
from the beginnings of his race when primitive man
felt that safety lay only in the destruction of the unknown. A thing he recognized for being the heritage
of the past, an emotion founded on fear rather than
intellect.

"John?" Bergman was impatient, and with reason.
If the thing was to be tried, it had to be done soon.
They had no time to waste.

"Go ahead," said Koenig, but qualified his agreement. "One chance only, Victor; we haven't time for
more. Unless Alan can divert the object, the other
Eagles will attempt to volatise and, if they fail, the
ground defences will take over. You've got two
minutes—make the most of them."

Alan Carter touched the controls and saw the target move on the screen, the fantastic shape steadying
on the cross-hairs of the sight. Beside him his co-
pilot checked the setting of the missile in the
launching tube.

"Primed and ready to go, Alan," he reported.
"Proximity fuse set for twenty—that's damned close."

It had to be close. In the void, explosions were
limited; without a medium to carry the shock wave,
their force was quickly dispersed and their destruc-

tive capabilities constrained. The missile in the
launching tube had a relatively minor charge as such
things went. A direct hit would turn half the target
into incandescent vapour and molten ruin—a near
miss would, so Bergman had calculated, send a blast
of ravening energy against the body and its surrounding, a thrust that would shift the bulk from its
line of flight. The difference between success and failure was small. Detonated too far from the target, the
blast would be insufficiently powerful to achieve the
desired result; too close, and it would destroy what he
was trying to save.

"Fifteen seconds," said Kano from the speaker.
"Computer is tracking."

Chad Bailey tensed in the co-pilot's seat. He was
young, intense, excited by the adventure even as he
was regretful at what had to be done. Rather than fire
the missile, he would have preferred to make physical
contact with the object, to touch it with his gloved
hands and to search for an entry if one existed.

"Alan—"

"Stand by to fire." Carter dropped a hand to the
control. "Mark?"

"Five," said Chad obediently as he watched the
hand of a chronometer. "Three . . . two . . . one . . .
fire!"

The Eagle jerked a trifle as the missile spat from
its tube, a metal dart tipped with destruction and riding a column of flame. Alan Carter knew his job and
had aimed well. He blinked as a gush of blue-white
flame filled the screens, a searing release of raw energy born in the heart of exploding atoms. It expanded like a flower to send a hail of photons and
atomic particles against the target.

"God, Alan! Look at that!"

Bailey leaned forward as he stared at the screen.
Around the enigmatic body of the strange object the
delicate lace-like surrounding was blazing with
trapped and reflected radiance. A mesh that had
caught the blast of energy, had responded to it as a

web would trap and reflect flame, dying in beauty even as it burned.

"It's beautiful," whispered Chad. "Beautiful!"

Carter said nothing, but his hands were shaking a little as he maintained control of the Eagle. The blast, though tremendously diminished, had caught and affected the ship.

"Alan?" Bergman spoke from the screen. "We saw the flash. Is everything as I hoped?"

"I think so, Professor. The target is undamaged as far as I can tell. That is, aside from some fusing of the surrounding structure." Carter expanded the magnification of his viewing screen. "About two-thirds gone, I'd say. Complete volatisation."

"The body itself?"

"Intact and apparently unharmed." Carter added, "Professor, there's something else we could try. Now that the surrounding has been burned away, we could try a direct push with the Eagle."

"No, Alan, it wouldn't work." Bergman was coldly precise. "I'd thought of that, but the mass is too great for you to affect it in any gainful manner. It would be like an ant trying to move a brick. A crude comparison, I admit, but a valid one. That object is far more dense and massive than it seems."

Material adamantine enough to resist the blast of an atomic missile, strong enough to have survived the vicissitudes of space. How long had it been travelling? What suns had it known, what worlds had it passed? From where had it come and, unless they had found it, where would it have ended?

Questions he knew could have no relevant answers. The thing was here, it had threatened Alpha and, for all he knew, was still threatening it.

Chad Bailey had the same thought.

"Was it enough, Alan? Should we have used another missile?"

"I don't know."

"Would it do any good if we had?" Bailey was pensive. "Could we destroy that thing even if we wanted to? Alan—"

"I don't know," said Carter again and added grimly, "All we can do now is to wait."

Once years ago David Kano had taken the first step on the road that was to lift him from a deprived area to the heights of Moonbase Alpha. For him at that time it had been far from easy, a matter of endless study after work that had numbed his muscles with physical weariness, poring over books while his contemporaries had been gaining what pleasure they could, relaxing at least, laughing and riding with the tide. To them he was a freak, a bookworm with stars in his eyes.

Only Frank Baker had recognised his idealism. "You've got ambition," he'd said. "But that isn't enough, David. With it you've got to have guts. You'll climb, but never think it's going to be easy. At times you'll get tired and want to quit. There'll be temptations and doubts, but remember always that what's worth having has to be worked for. You need dedication and application and, above all, patience."

Old Frank Baker, dead now, planted in some ancient ground or burned for his ashes to mingle with the soil he had loved. A gardener at Savannah High. A man who could barely read, but who'd held more wisdom in the tip of a finger than many libraries.

"Patience," he'd said. "You have to learn to wait."

But waiting had never been easy. Not then when he'd sat in a darkened room waiting for the results of his first examination. Nor later when he'd made application to join the personnel of Moonbase Alpha. Not now when he waited for Computer to deliver the answer of whether they were to live or die.

An exaggeration, perhaps. The commander, he knew, had taken precautions, but the thing was alien and it was barely possible that not even the fury of atomic power could volatise it into a harmless, diffusing vapour. Even though fused, shapeless, and an amorphous mass scintillant with radioactive energy, it could still follow the path fate had dictated, to land as previously predicted and kill everyone on the Moon.

Mass, he thought, bleakly. No matter what shape it takes, energy is still mass. A moving body held kinetic energy, which gave it the potential danger of a bomb. He could ask Computer to give him the figures, but what good would they do? It was better, if they were doomed, not to know of the coming end.

"Kano!"

He blinked and became suddenly aware of the tension reigning in Main Mission, the attention directed towards himself. He had been dreaming, remembering, then he realised that the time that had seemed so long hadn't been that at all. There was no read-out as yet from the computer. It was merely that Koenig was impatient.

"Kano," he said again. "Anything yet?"

"Give it time, John," said Bergman mildly. "The new course has to be plotted."

"If there is a new course."

"There will be if my calculations were correct."

Bergman was still mild. "Try to relax, John. Mathematics is an exact science."

And one of which he was a master, but always there was the possibility of error, and they were dealing with the unknown. Koenig turned and paced the floor, turning again as he reached the wall to head back towards the main console. A mistake; his movements were causing a distraction and adding to the general tension. He forced himself to halt and appear at ease.

Theoretically they were safe. The mathematics promised that and, yet, how to be certain? A relatively minor force correctly applied to a moving object could divert it from its original path. The touch of a leaf against a rifle bullet as it left the muzzle could send it off-target—if the leaf were strong enough and the bullet light enough. It all depended on relative mass.

"Kano?" Surely the computer would have the answer by now?

"Nothing as yet, Commander. I—" The technician broke off as a signal lamp flashed and a slip of paper appeared in the read-out slot. "Here it is now." His voice rose as, tearing free the slip, he read the data it contained. "We've done it! We're safe!"

"The figures?"

"The divergence from the previous flight path is almost a tenth of a second of arc. The new point of impact will be about thirty miles from Alpha in the region of Schemiel."

A shallow crater thick with accumulated dust. Koenig said sharply, "There is no doubt?"

"None."

"Make a double check. Paul, have the Eagles stand by to be ready for emergency action. Have Carter track the object and relay his findings."

"Yes, Commander. The Red Alert?"

"To be maintained until impact."

Which would be in about eight minutes from now. Koenig glanced at the big face of the chronometer, a part of his brain wondering at the relative speeds of the passage of time. Minutes ago he had been watching the delicate play of water from a fountain, and yet it seemed like hours since he had stood in the new cavern. And now, he knew, time would seem to slow down, each second crawling past, each minute a seeming eternity until the object had landed and he could be sure the Moonbase was safe.

"Report from Eagle One confirms the new impact point," said Kano from his station at the computer. "A one-mile circle centered on Schemiel."

"Probable results?"

"Some minor tremors. The dust should soften the impact and it's a long way from Alpha."

Koenig felt himself relax, the muscles easing in his arms and stomach, the tension dissolving from the nape of his neck. He caught Bergman's eye and smiled and said, "You've done it again, Victor."

"I had time to think, John," said the professor. "You had to take care of the Moonbase. I could have been wrong, in which case your precautions would have saved us." He looked at the screen on which the object was now clearly visible, the following Eagle a watchful guardian. "A visitor," he mused. "Something made and sent into space."

"You can't be sure of that."

"No, but those vanes, that tracery, the shape itself —how could it be rock? There is a symmetry about it, a design. Form, John, is the result of function, as you well know. Certain products have to be the shape they are in order to fulfill their function—they couldn't operate if shaped any other way. A wheel is a classic example. What else could it be but round? And a hammer—no matter how crude the construction, the basic design is the same, a weight on the end of a shaft. A shape inevitable to the function of the tool and one that tells the use to which it is put. Logically, from the shape and size of that object, we should be able to tell what it is and from where it came." He added anxiously, "Have photographs been taken?"

"Of course." Koenig smiled. "More than enough for you to use at your lecture."

"What lecture?" Bergman frowned, then, smiling, shrugged. "Sorry, John, but I was getting carried away. Old, too, I guess, and forgetful."

Koenig dismissed Bergman's statement with a wave. He glanced down at the chronometer again. "Just over a minute to go now, Victor." And to Morrow he said, "Recall all Eagles. Have them hover over Moonbase until after the impact."

"No observation?"

"None." The thing could detonate on landing. Any hovering Eagle would be caught in a gush of fire like a moth trapped in a flame. "Void the area."

"It's coming," said a girl. "Look!"

It showed now in the direct-vision screens, a small mass dimly lit by starlight, turning a little as it slanted across the sky. From her instruments Sandra Benes began counting seconds.

"Fifty-two, fifty-one, fifty . . . no sign of any emitted radiation. No differential in temperature. Some residual radioactivity."

From the blast of the atomic missile, naturally, but it could only be negligible.

"Impact point ten yards from northern lip of Schemiel," said Kano quietly.

Bergman was sharp. "On the rock?"

"Yes, Professor."

"John! It'll be wrecked!"

"That or lost," agreed Koenig. "But there's nothing we can do about it."

"Twenty-three," said Sandra. "Twenty-two, twenty-one, twenty, nineteen . . . "

"Sound impact warning," snapped Koenig, and as Morrow obeyed and the siren echoed throughout the Moonbase, he leaned forward as if actual closeness to the window could give him better vision, which was blocked, since thick steel plates rose to protect the glass to seal Main Mission against all danger of breakage and resultant air loss.

"Seven." Sandra's voice was tense, as was the atmosphere in Main Mission. "Three, two, one—now!"

A moment of frozen stillness and then, on her instruments, lights flashed, signals followed almost immediately by a dull rumble, the slight shifting of the floor beneath their feet.

A moment that Koenig ignored. "Paul?"

Morrow was already busy, hands darting over his console as screen after screen lit up, each section reporting a total lack of any damage.

"Base secure, Commander," he finally reported. "All systems at optimum. No damage, no casualties. Normal procedure?"

Koenig nodded, sensing the relief of tension as the Red Alert was terminated, the life of Alpha resuming its normal path. The threat from space had been faced, dealt with, and averted without damage, as had been reported.

But Paul had been wrong when he'd stated there had been no casualties.

Lynne Saffery had gone insane.

CHAPTER THREE

She lay on the bed, writhing, snarling, her face like that of an animal. Koenig stared down at her; a young and attractive girl who had suddenly turned into a beast. Froth edged her lips and her body arched beneath the straps that held her down firmly. Her hands, curved, drove her nails into the palms. Beside her Helena checked a hypodermic syringe and touched it to the corded throat.

As the girl quietened he said, "What happened?"

"I don't know. We were running a series of experiments to determine the strength of her paraphysical attributes. I had just sedated her to achieve full relaxation when you warned me about the Yellow Alert. She was asleep, apparently harmless, and I just didn't worry anymore about her." Helena's hand lifted to touch her throat. Against the smooth pearl of her skin, bruises showed in ugly blotches. "As it turned out, that was a mistake."

"She attacked you?"

"Yes."

"When?"

"Shortly after the Red Alert. I was at my desk when

I heard a soft noise behind me. Or maybe I just sensed something. As I rose she grabbed me. If it hadn't been for my training—" Helena broke off and shook her head. "She was tremendously strong, but that I can understand. Hysteria can cause that and the more so when coupled with mania, but she was resting, sedated and asleep. And there is no previous history of any kind of aberration. She is just a normal, typical, level-headed girl."

Once, perhaps, but not now. Koenig leaned forward and eased the fingers from where they dug into the palms. Little crescents of red showed, wounds that quickly filled with blood.

"You'll have to trim her nails," he said absently. "Could your experiments have had anything to do with her breakdown?"

"No." Helena saw his expression and elaborated. "We were running through a series of tests with the five cards—those devised by Dr Rhine years ago. Her scores were high at times, low at others, and it was obvious that her talent lay in telepathy. Only when I looked at the cards could she gain a high score. It seemed plain that she was reading the image from my mind. I checked her out on a few other runs, making sure I didn't see the designs, for example, turning the cards after a certain interval; but only when I looked at them before she gave the answer did she make a high score. To me it was a clear indication of mental rapport."

"And?"

"I'd only touched the surface and wanted to probe deeper. With her permission I intended to record her brain wave pattern before, during and after a test."

"You told me she'd been sedated," reminded Koenig. "Asleep, you said."

"Technically, yes," she admitted. "But there are different varieties of sleep, John. I had her on the upper level of the first stage of hypnotic trance. She would have been able to hear my voice and to respond to instruction but, at the same time, being totally relaxed.

After you'd given the Yellow Alert, I let her slide into unconsciousness—as I said, I couldn't see it doing any harm."

A sleep from which the girl had awakened in a killing frenzy. But why? Dr Mathias shrugged as Koenig asked the question. He had come to join the commander and Helena.

"There's no clear-cut textbook answer, Commander. If pressed I'd say that the possibility of someone waking from sleep in a maniacal state of murderous frenzy is so remote as to be negligible. For a normal person to make such a sudden switch is, I would say, impossible, not without some form of external influence."

"Such as?"

"Drugs, hypnotic suggestion, induced hallucination, extensive cranial manipulation—"

"Surgery?"

"In one form or another, yes. The human being is a very tough character, Commander. It doesn't go from sanity to insanity in a flash without a very good reason."

One they would have to find . . . what could affect one person could affect another and, in the close confines of Alpha, such mysteries could not be ignored.

Helena said quietly, "I've already taken full precautionary measures, John. And tests are being made on the girl to determine if any virus or bacteria could have been responsible for her mental breakdown. As yet all findings are negative." Pausing, she added, "Physical ones, at least."

"And mental?"

In response she wheeled forward a machine that stood against the wall at the head of the couch. Wires ran from it, each tipped with a small adhesive pad. Deftly she attached them to various points on the limp girl's skull.

"I told you that I'd been about to make brain wave recordings of Lynne's mind during the tests I'd devised. I'd attached her to the machine as I have now, and everything was ready to go when I received your Yellow Alert. Now, something must have happened. A convulsion of some kind, perhaps, or a natural movement; in either case, Lynne must have accidentally switched on the machine. She could have done it like this." Helena lifted one of the limp hands, swung it from the bed, let it fall. A finger hit a switch and threw it with a soft click. "See?"

Koenig looked at the blank screen. "It isn't working."

"Because I haven't engaged the visual, but it was on then and will be in a moment. First I want you to watch this." An adjustment and the screen flared to life, an intricate pattern of lines rippling across the surface. "Lynne Saffery's brain wave pattern as recorded a month ago. Normal, Bob, don't you agree?"

Mathias said dryly, "If it hadn't been normal, the girl would have been hospitalised long ago."

"Exactly. Now, John, look at this." The screen flickered as Helena adjusted a control, took on the familiar pattern, then flickered again to reveal one distorted almost beyond recognition. "The recording made while Lynne was attached to the machine during the alert. At first normal, then a sudden change. It shifts, varies, holds steady, then shifts again to finally settle into this." The distortion held, lines writhing across the screen, then abruptly the screen went blank. "That was when she rose and broke the connection. Now look at this. A direct recording this time, one taken at this very moment from her brain."

Koenig looked at the distorted pattern. The array of intricate lines seemed to hold a disquietening menace, a disturbing implication that he lacked the skill to understand.

Mathias came to his aid.

"It's alien," he said bleakly. "A combination I've never seen originating in a human brain before this moment. The alpha rhythm is all wrong, and the beta is totally inhuman. And look at this." His finger lifted to rest on the screen. "This line here. I've seen it only once before when we were doing research into animal behaviour at the Kenyatta Institute at Nairobi. We were using monkeys with implanted electrodes to determine the various motor regions of the cortex. Old stuff, but always there are new students and the director had his own ideas of how to teach them. Some of us grew bored and tried an experiment of our own. We had an old encephalograph and an electronic genius who souped it up to use direct-beam contact. He managed to focus it on an insect, a spider."

"And?"

"That's when I saw that pattern." Mathias touched it again. "It was a freak, we could never repeat it, but I don't think any of us there ever forgot it."

"And the line?" Helena glanced at it, then back to Mathias. "Did you determine what it signified?"

"Yes," he said shortly. "Hunger."

One day, thought Bergman, they would invent a mobile capsule of air so that they could sit within it and be wafted like bubbles over the Lunar plain. But that day hadn't yet arrived and survival still depended on encompassing suits that clung to body and limbs, making each step an effort despite the lower gravity. Within the confines of his helmet he could hear the soft hiss of air, an irritation at times, but one designed to save life. While he could hear the air he was safe; when he couldn't, death was coming close. A stuck valve, an empty tank, a small tear in the suit—any of a dozen things that would terminate the existence of a creature that had ventured too far from the warmth and comfort of its own domain.

"Professor?" Alan Carter was speaking from the Eagle, which he and the others of the party had just left. "You're sure that you don't want me to drop you smack on the spot?"

"And have your rockets blast dust over everything?" Bergman shook his head, forgetting that the other couldn't see the gesture, could only hear his voice over the inter-suit radio. He and the others, nat-

urally, and those back at Alpha who would be monitoring the little expedition. "Thanks, Alan, but no.
We've been over this before."

A battle that he had won as, logically, he had to
win. Insisting on all care being taken that nothing
should be lost, that every scrap of the wrecked object
be found for later examination. If it was wrecked, of
course—could a mass of rock be wrecked? A point
Koenig had made when, shrugging, he had let
Bergman have his own way.

"Just be careful, Victor," he'd warned, "and watch
the dust."

The fine, so very fine dust that could swallow a man
as if it had been water—the reason he and the others
were roped together as if they had been mountaineers.

A dozen more steps and he stood on a rising edge to
halt and stare over the Lunar terrain. To all sides the
surface was pocked and seamed, torn by ancient erup-
tions or savaged by celestial rain; the impact of me-
teorites that had left their traces in gaping craters, the
internal strains that had cracked the surface as if it
had been glass struck with a gigantic hammer.

A scene of stark, awesome beauty. Cold, hostile,
grey and white and silver beneath the starlight, shadows thick like solid masses where no light could reach.

Home.

Home!

"Which way, Professor?" A figure raised an arm and
pointed. "I can see something over there." The voice
hesitated. "Something spiny, I think."

A trick of the starlight, it had to be—the lace-like
surrounding of the enigmatic body could never have
withstood the shock of impact; but even so, Bergman
felt a rising hope. Too often, he'd found, the old,
safe, familiar laws no longer applied. Here, in the
depths of the galaxy, far from the region in which he
had been born, waited odd surprises.

"Professor?"

"No." He must remain logical. "Head more to the

west. We should see a gap in the rim-wall of Schemiel soon and, when we do, head towards it."

The little party moved on, ants crawling over the face of creation, reaching the broken rim-wall and climbing to halt and stare at what lay below.

"Look at that!" The voice was incredulous. "Just look at it!"

"Luck!" Another sucked in his breath. "Well, we've found it."

Or what was left of it. Bergman stared at the sloping wall of the crater, the shattered stone, the twisted mass lying in the cold light of the stars. A ship, he thought dully; no mass of rock could ever have broken in such a fashion. And yet, even while he stared, he knew that it wasn't a ship, that it could never have been a vessel fashioned by intelligence for traversing space.

"This is crazy," said a voice from the radio. "What the hell is it?"

A mystery that lay sprawled and broken in the silver glow thrown by remote suns. The delicate, lace-like fabrication of the surrounding had gone, ripped and torn, shattered and broken, scraps and fragments spread over the entire area. The body itself had struck the rim-wall, smashing stone, lunging through to come to rest on the far side.

Not a ship and not a mass of stone or mineral. Not solid at all.

"It's like a shell," said a man wonderingly. "A pod of some kind. Split open and twisted."

And empty—if it had ever been filled.

Bergman walked alongside it as technicians busied themselves taking photographs and measurements. They worked with an easy casualness; now that it had landed, the thing wouldn't leave and, in a century, a millennia, it would still be as they saw it now. Without wind or rain or the abrasion of weather, things left on the surface were eternal.

Bergman kicked at a fragment of oddly shaped material and held it close to his face-plate. His helmet light shone on a peculiar crystalline structure, little glints showing in a field of ebon. A part of the shattered surrounding, perhaps? A portion of that enigmatic lattice that must have served a purpose, but if so, one that would probably never be known.

Tucking the fragment into a sack, he moved on. A rise of debris rested against the shattered side of the split object and he climbed it to reach the lip and to stare inside. The speaker who had likened it to a pod had been correct; the thing gave that impression and added to it with the subtle curves of the interior. Even allowing for the distortion that could have been caused by the landing, it was obvious that the inside of the object had been hollow and that no line had been straight.

A hull tough enough to withstand the blast of an atomic missile. Vanes like lace that had served no apparent purpose. A hollow interior that defied all rational explanation. Material that lay beyond his knowledge.

"Professor?" One of the men called over the radio. "What do you want us to do?"

"Spread out," said Bergman, "and look."

A technician was the first to find one. He tripped and fell to rise, cursing, rubbing at an elbow even as he checked his suit.

Then his voice broke, to rise, to echo from Bergman's radio. "Professor! Come and take a look at this!"

It was lying half-buried in dust, rolled free by the impact of a boot to lie in a patch of shadow cast by a fret of stone. Something that glinted as if made of silver, which coruscated with a brilliant profusion of light as he held it in the beam of his helmet. Something that looked like a ball.

It was the size of a grapefruit, the skin with a metallic sheen, whorled like a thumbprint, the delicate engraving catching and diffusing the light so that it glowed like a rainbow.

"What the hell is it?" The technician who had kicked it nursed his foot. "I've never seen anything like that on the Moon before. And it's heavy. I damned near busted my foot on it."

Its Earth-weight, Bergman calculated, would be about that of lead. A sixth as much here on the Moon, but still too much for him to manage with one hand even had the size allowed him to obtain a grip. He rose with it cradled in both palms.

"Listen," he said into the radio. "Attention, all of you." He described the object he held. "There could be others, and if so, they are probably lying around and in front of the wreck. Please look for them. They may be almost buried in the dust or they could be lying in shadow. Shine light on the ground and you will see the reflection. It is unmistakable. Please concentrate your search as of now on the recovery of these objects."

The technician who had found the one Bergman held said curiously, "What are they, Professor? Gems of some kind?"

"I doubt it."

"Then what?" The man was no fool. "Minerals, then? Nodules like those of magnesium found on the ocean beds back home?"

"Perhaps."

"Of lead or platinum, maybe?" The man reached out and touched the sphere. His gloved fingers ran over the fine markings. "Perhaps the impact of that thing opened up a vein of some sort. We could have found a mine of sorts. Right, Prof?"

"Perhaps," said Bergman. "Now, how about looking for more?"

The next was found within two minutes, the third immediately afterwards, and within an hour they had a heap of them piled like ancient cannonballs to one side of the wreck.

And it had to be a wreck, of that Bergman was now certain, but the wreck of *what* he had no idea.

Sliding down the inside of one half of the shattered,

pod-like thing, he made his way towards a technician busy with a cutting torch. The beam of the laser hit the material the man was working on, seeming to be absorbed in it, the fierce concentration of heat having no noticeable effect.

"Useless." The man cut the torch. "This stuff soaks up energy like a sponge, yet it looks hard enough." His gloved hand rapped against the smooth surface. "And it had to be worked to get this finish. See how it gleams?" He illustrated with his light. "That takes grinding with a fine abrasive—take my word for it."

"Can you cut it with a saw?"

"Frank's trying." A hand lifted to where a man crouched on the edge of the hollowed shell working with something that glittered. "Hey, Frank! Any luck as yet?"

"Not much," said a disgruntled voice from the radio. "Saws were useless, so now I'm trying a wheel."

"What are you using?" said Bergman. "Emery?"

"I've tried emery; it was useless. Now I'm on a diamond wheel, and if this can't do it I'm giving up."

"Any progress?"

"Some, but it's mighty slow. I'll be lucky to get a small wedge cut free before the wheel wears out. Well —it's a way to pass the time."

Bergman moved on. The men could work as well without his supervision, and his presence would only irritate them, as their presence would him if he were engaged in an experiment. Dropping from the rear of the wreck, the part that had hit last and called the rear only because of that, he stepped back to gain a wider view.

It was of little help. Behind him lay the crater of Schemiel, the dust that almost filled it marked by the scars of passage. The alien object had hit, bounced from the dust as a stone would bounce when skipped over water and smashed hard against the rim-wall. It had broken through and had slid partly down the far slope.

Had it split open on first landing, on hitting the rim-wall or when finally coming to rest? The two halves, warped and twisted, lay close. The common join showed a clean break without any trace of sheared components or torn stanchions.

A deliberately designed fracture plane?

If so—why?

Musing, Bergman stepped backwards and, too late, recognised his danger. His foot, instead of landing on solid ground, plunged into a bottomless lack of resistance. Desperately he threw himself forward, hands clawing at the rock, his fingers finding a hold and clamping hard to it as slowly he drew his foot out of the dust and heaved himself to safety.

A momentary danger quickly passed, but a moment of carelessness that could have been fatal. Once buried in the dust, the chances of rescue were remote and, if the dust was deep, impossible.

"Victor?" Koenig spoke from the radio. "How are you going? Victor?"

"Here, John." Bergman drew in a deep breath and forced his voice to sound calm. "Fine."

"Have you solved the mystery yet? You've had long enough."

"Yes, John, I have."

"What?" Koenig had been joking. Now he was incredulous. "You know what that thing was and what it carried?"

"Yes." Bergman paused, enjoying his moment. "It was a pod, John, and it carried seeds."

CHAPTER FOUR

Bergman's quarters were adorned with the past; fragments of ancient civilisations, yellowed journals, old books, faded scraps of tapestry. On a wall hung his awards, among them the Nobel Prize, but there were no photographs of friends he had known or relations he would never see again. The past, to Bergman, was as much a tool as the slide rules lying on his desk, the delicately calibrated instruments in his laboratory. A thing to be used, to remind him of what had been, an illustration of what could be accomplished. Steps by which mankind had lifted itself from the mud to the stars.

Koenig liked the room and was often to be found there with his old friend. But now he had not come to play chess or to talk or to simply sit and relax away the never-ending duties of his command.

"Seeds," he said. "Victor, are you sure?"

"No, John, I am not." Bergman was carefully precise. "There are few things about which anyone can be totally certain, but the probability that I am correct is high. Everything leads towards it—the shape of the pod, the surrounding, the way it split, the strange spheres we found."

"An assumption."

"Of course, John, but without actual proof, what else can we have?"

"But, seeds?"

"It's possible, John." Helena had been looking at a sketch of an old house, one that Bergman had hoped to build and never had. "Think of the seed pods we knew back home—the sycamore seeds with their propeller-like motion, the drifting puffs from thistles and dandelions, those plants that seem to literally fire their seeds into the air by the release of coiled springs."

"Yes, but the size?"

"Size is relative. Think of a coconut; that is a tremendously large seed when compared to an acorn, and an acorn is huge when compared to a beechnut. And there are seeds so small they can hardly be seen with the naked eye. I think Victor could be right, John. That object we found could have been a pod sent into space somehow and drifted until it found somewhere to rest."

"Such as?"

"How can I be sure? Another world, perhaps, or even a region of space that would trigger it to life. I'm a physician, John, not a botanist, but I'll bet there are vegetative life-cycles similar in pattern, if not in size."

She looked, he thought, very lovely as she stood, the light gleaming from her hair, the firm yet soft contours of her body a continual reminder of the woman she was and the femininity she exuded. And it pleased him to play the devil's advocate, to argue against something his intelligence had already told him was more than probable and certainly more than possible.

"Let's be rational about this, Helena. You, too, Victor. First the size—what manner of tree could produce a seed pod twice the size of an Eagle plus a surrounding tracery? And why the tracery? We know that the mass of the thing was too great for it to have been driven by light-pressure."

"Wind, perhaps?" Bergman frowned, thinking. "A sudden rush of air, assuming the planet of origin had a low gravity, would have caught the tracery and used it as a sail to lift the thing up and into space. Also, the size tends to the conclusion that it came from some low-gravity world. The size of plants is limited by their ability to pump water up from the roots to the topmost branches. A moment."

A projector stood on a desk and Bergman activated it, light and colour flashing to illuminate a screen. Against the familiar backdrop of stars, the enigmatic object rested like a rare and precious jewel.

"Taken before the initial laser-blast," said Bergman. "One of an entire series of photographs and as good as any to illustrate my meaning. Study the tracery. You see that the veins are convoluted, which gives the structure a tremendous surface area in relation to its actual size. A pity that it couldn't have been preserved intact; our topologists would have had a field day in plotting the curves and vectors, but we can still gain some information. Now, assuming a steady force of wind, what pressures would be needed to move the entire mass against, say, zero gravity?"

"High," said Koenig. "We had to use the blast of an atomic missile to shift it, remember?"

"We used it," corrected Bergman. "But we didn't have to. Given time we could have found an alternative. Also remember that, without a conducting medium, no blast can have a high shock wave. An explosion in water will create a more violent shock wave than one in the atmosphere—the denser the medium, the greater the transmission. The pod need not have originated in space; in fact, I tend to think the facts are against it. A large, but low-gravity world, perhaps one subjected to violent storms, one that could have an intensely active sun remitting tremendous amounts of radiation."

"A combination sufficient to send a pod into the

void," said Helena. "As the explosion of Krakatoa in 1883 created a hole a thousand feet in depth in the ocean and blasted debris into space. An accident, Victor?"

"The pod? Perhaps not, Helena."

Koenig said, "Arrhenius?"

"Why not, John?" Bergman met his eyes. "Why not?"

Koenig made no answer, thinking of the man they had mentioned, his very name encompassing a theory that, at the time of its mention, shook minds with its calm acceptance of the fact that life in the universe need not be confined to one world. Professor Svante August Arrhenius, who had proposed the possibility that life in the form of spores could be carried throughout the galaxy, even throughout the entire universe, by the pressure of light. Minute scraps of potential life—seeds—swept through the void until, attracted by the gravitational well of a possible home, they had fallen to their fate. To live or to die. To spread life or to wither in pools of acid, fires, seas of noxious liquids, corrosive gases or frigid wastes.

"Spores," said Koenig. "But this—" He broke off, gesturing at the screen.

"Size is relative, John," reminded Helena. "To an ant we are mobile mountains, and to a bacteria an ant is a world."

A fact he knew and he was tired of playing the devil's advocate. To argue the opposing side was often necessary in order to bring into the open facts that could be too easily overlooked or deliberately ignored. And he had known what Bergman wanted from the first.

"I want to plant them, John. The seeds, I mean, I want to see if they will grow."

"If they are seeds."

"I'm positive they are." Bergman switched off the projector and led the way into his small laboratory. On a bench rested a seed, sliced open, the halves lying side by side. "I managed to cut one open using a sonic drill and vibratory wire," he explained. "I wrapped the wire around the sphere, constricting it as I vibrated it with the drill. Tedious, but it worked." He handed a section to Helena, another to Koenig. "Look at it and tell me what you see."

A mass of closely packed substance more familiar to Helena than to Koenig.

"Victor!" Her voice was incredulous. "This looks like compacted tissue!"

Koenig said, "Animal or vegetable?"

"Without microscopic examination there is no way to tell. Have you tested it, Victor?"

"Yes, but without definite results," he admitted. "But one thing is certain—it is molecular, not crystalline. There is a regular cell-like structure and nodes that could carry the genetic nucleus. The overall pattern is that of a seed. The pod in which it travelled places it in the vegetable kingdom. John, I want your permission to plant them."

"In Alpha?"

"Where else?" Bergman was insistent. "We can use the new rural area. It's ideal for the purpose. No crops have been planted there yet, and we have a perfect environment—artificial sunlight that can be varied, water, air, a regulated temperature. John, you can't refuse!"

He could and should if there was the slightest risk of endangering the Moonbase, but always progress had to be attended by a calculated gamble. And, if they were to learn, chances had to be taken.

"Think of what it could mean if we can cultivate them, John," urged Bergman. "That pod out there, it's the hardest thing we've found. Not even a diamond wheel can cut it easily. It's proof against a laser. If we can learn how to utilise it, we'll have a new building material. And there could be more. Who knows what the seeds may give us if they can be persuaded to grow?"

"All right, Victor," said Koenig. "Go ahead."

It was a decision made as all decisions had to be made—a matter of compromise and a searching for the best for the least effort and the lowest risk. To deny the Moonbase the potential gain of the seeds was to go beyond his function, for a commander should lead and guide, not use his position to be dictatorial. And yet Koenig wouldn't have been human if he was absolved from all doubt.

"You had no choice, John," said Helena as he later accompanied her to Medical Centre. "We need what those seeds could give, and how could you have denied Victor his opportunity to probe into something so entrancing?"

"He isn't a child, Helena. He doesn't need a toy."

"But he needs to keep his mind exercised, John. We all do." Abruptly serious, she halted and turned to face him, oblivious of the others present in the corridor. "Surely you know the edge we all are riding on. Strain can be absorbed only to a certain degree. Maintain an artificial way of life and trouble is inevitable. Couple the strain of unaccustomed living with the fear of personal extinction and we have a situation the same as was present in the trenches during World War One. Later they called it combat fatigue, and we know it as the General Adaption Syndrome. People can only stand so much for so long—maintain the pressure and things begin to happen, nasty things including murder, violence and sudden death."

And rape and quarrels and sudden, apparently illogical, outbursts of verbal and physical violence. Koenig had known it all back in the past when too many people had been crowded into too few rooms, tenements teeming with life on the verge of explosion. Emotions that had blazed out in riots and burnings, savage, wanton destruction and a sickly suicidal impulse to kill and kill until killed in turn. In the East they had known it as running amok.

He never wanted to see it happen in Alpha.

Helena was one who would take care that it did not. With her tests and programmes devised to maintain harmony, with selective sedations and continual monitoring of all personnel, always ready to quench the fires before they could blaze, recognising the smoke for what it was.

And yet, even so, Lynne Saffery had gone insane.

"I don't know why, John," Helena confessed when he asked. "As far as we can determine, there is no trace of any organic cause. Her cortex is free of any sign of a tumor, there is no question of radiation sickness and her physical condition is excellent. The only real fact on which we can work is her encephalogram."

"The line that Bob said denoted hunger?"

"Yes."

"You've checked?"

"Yes." She hesitated. "That is, we've tried. One of the attendants volunteered to act as a guinea pig. He's been starving himself, but it's too early to tell as yet whether a similar line will appear on his encephalogram. Personally, I don't think that it will."

"Which proves what?"

"Perhaps nothing. Or perhaps the machine was at fault. It could have been affected by some external source and given a jumbled reading."

"In which case the girl isn't really ill at all," he said dryly. "She only thinks that she is because the machine tells her so. Am I making sense, Helena?"

"Yes, if she had seen the machine and knew just what the record signified. Stranger things have happened, John, especially to susceptible people. But she didn't see the records, so your theory can't apply. In any case, her symptoms aren't appropriate to a self-induced state of hysterical mania. Do you want to see her?"

She looked very small as she lay on the bed, her knees drawn up a little, her shoulders curved in a near-foetal position. On her cheeks her eyelashes rested like ebon moths and her hair, neatly arranged, framed the contours of her face as if it were a painting done by an artist of the pre-Raphaelite school. An angel, Koenig thought, but, at times, all men thought women were angels. Most later changed their minds.

"Lynne?" Helena touched the smooth curve of the girl's cheek. "Lynne?" She looked up as Mathias came toward them. "Is she still under sedation?"

"It should be passing now." He glanced at his watch, then at the clipped papers at the foot of the bed. "Yes, another dose about due."

Koenig said, "Does she have to be under continual sedation?"

"We've tried letting her come out of it and we had to use restraints," explained Helena. "When she began to show signs of muscular hypertension, we had to take action. She would have wound up by breaking her own bones," she explained. "Like a person poisoned with strychnine—the muscular convulsions override the mental safety factor. It's kinder to keep her under sedation."

"For how long?"

"Until we can find the cause of her trouble and eliminate it. Are you ready, Doctor?"

Mathias nodded and checked his hypodermic syringe. As the girl stirred on the bed, Koenig said sharply, "Wait!"

"John?"

"I want to see what happens. Let her come out of it." He leaned over the bed. "Lynne? Can you hear me? Wake up, Lynne. Wake up!"

"Commander!" She smiled like a sleepy child, soft, warm, comfortable. "John Koenig. I'm in love with you, John, did you know that? I've always been in love with you." She turned and lifted her arms to embrace him, holding him fast about the neck as she pulled his head down towards her own. "But I'm so hungry, John," she continued in a thin, whining tone. "So very hungry. Feed me, John. Feed me! Feed me!"

Her arms became circlets of steel, her mouth, open, a ruby-tinted cavern in which shone the whiteness of her teeth—teeth that tore at his throat, breaking the skin, freeing blood that stained her lips, her chin, ran to dapple the smooth roundness of her shoulders.

"Lynne!" Helena's hand moved, flattened, the palm rammed over the gaping mouth, fingers and thumb upcurved safe from the snapping teeth. "Bob! Quickly!"

Mathias needed no urging. He stooped, the hypodermic syringe in his hand darting towards the column of the girl's throat, his finger triggering the mechanism that shot the drug into her bloodstream. A moment and then the arms that had been locked around Koenig's neck fell away as, sighing, the girl lapsed into sedated rest.

To Alan Carter an Eagle was an extension of his being; its engines a supplement to his own physical power, its armament a strengthening of his muscles, the computer maintaining its efficiency an actual part of his brain. Once in the control chair he became one with the machine, an attribute that had made him the finest pilot of his time and that had made him the head of his section. As the chief pilot of Reconnaissance, he was aware of his duties and responsibility.

As he was a part of the Eagle he flew, so also was he an extension of Alpha. Its long-range eyes and hands and brain. An essential part of the complex that kept them all alive. And, if sometimes his duties were routine, well, they had to be done. And, always, for him it was a pleasure to be handling an Eagle, even on such a minor task as this.

Beside him Chad Bailey said, "A milk run, Alan. A collection job."

"It could be worse."

"Sure, we could be down there grubbing in the dust for those things Bergman says are seeds. Seeds!" His snort was indicative of his feelings in the matter. "They look more like ball bearings to me. Say, how about that? Maybe that's what they really are. Some joke, eh? The professor trying to grow ball bearing trees."

Alan smiled. The joke was poor, but he'd heard worse, and Chad, while a little unthinking, knew his job. If he hadn't, he would never have been allowed to occupy the chair he did. Only the best could be trusted with an Eagle.

"Take over, Chad." Relinquishing the controls, Carter contacted the base. "Paul? Alan here. Eagle One now close to impact point. Any change in the orders?"

"No. Just pick up any of the spheres that may have been found and bring them back to Moonbase."

"The men, too?"

"Yes. Later we'll arrange to collect the wreckage and move it closer, but for now it'll do no harm where it is. How long will you be?"

"A few minutes. We're not hurrying. I'm taking a routine sweep over the area to spot any new fissures. As yet, nothing. I guess the impact was as soft as it seemed."

On the screen Morrow nodded. "Just as well for all of us. Things like that I can do without. Chess later on?"

"Sure, Paul. Care to bet?"

"What's the point? You always lose."

"Not this time. I've been——" Carter broke off as Morrow's face tensed. "Paul! Something wrong?"

"I'm not sure. I——Alan! Listen to this!"

It came from the speakers in a gurgling rush, voices trying to speak, to scream, to relay information, the whole lost in a sussurating blur of static. A background roar that blasted from the speakers like the rush of surf.

"It's coming from the impact site!" yelled Morrow. "Alan! Get there—fast!"

A few miles, the Eagle responding to his touch like a living thing, vapour blasting from the tubes, more streaming from the retro-rockets as the velocity was

cut and the Eagle set to hover as both pilots searched
the scarred terrain below.

"Nothing," said Chad. "I can't see a thing."

"Keep looking." Alan lowered the Eagle. "Those
men have to be somewhere."

The roar from the speakers had died, replaced by a
brooding silence, against which Morrow's voice rasped
with mounting urgency.

"Harmond! Chagny! Answer. If you read me, answer. Harmond! Chagny!"

Two men, neither responding, neither to be seen.
As Carter swept the Eagle over the impact area, Chad
drew in his breath, then almost immediately shook his
head.

"Nothing. I thought I saw a hint of movement, but
I guess it was our shadow passing over some rocks."

"Where?" Carter sent the Eagle to hover over the
place. Shadows were possible, patches of dimness
against the starlit rocks, but it would take extraordi-
nary eyes to spot the difference. "See anything?"

"No."

Imagination, then, the most likely explanation. But
there was none to account for the missing men.

"The dust," suggested Bailey. "Maybe they fell into
the dust."

"Both of them?"

"One could have slipped and the other tried to
save him. An outcrop of rock could have yielded and
cost him his balance. Both could have been swallowed
in a fraction of time." Pausing, he added, "Radios
don't work when deep under the dust."

A logical explanation, but Carter wasn't happy with
it. Both men had been experienced surface workers
and would have known better than to venture too
close to any patch of dust unless having first taken
all precautions. And if they had and one had slipped,
the other would have been able to save him. Certainly
he would have had time to make a report.

"Alan?" Morrow looked from the screen. "Any
luck?"

"No. Both men have vanished. Bailey thinks they fell into the dust."

"He could be right."

"Shall we land and search?"

"No!" Koenig replaced Morrow on the screen. "Don't land on any account. Return and pick up a search party."

"But those men, Commander. They could be hurt, maybe dying."

"If so I don't want you to join them." Koenig's voice matched the hardness of his face. "Do as I order. Return immediately and pick up a search party. I'll have it waiting."

He was suited and with a dozen others on the loading dock when the Eagle arrived. Without wasting time they thronged into the passenger module, Koenig moving forward as the Eagle lifted and headed back the way it had come.

"Commander!" Carter handed the controls over to Bailey. "Your orders?"

"None until I know what's happened. Did you see anything? Anything at all?"

"No. Bailey thought he saw something move, but it must have been a shadow. We looked but saw nothing."

"Where was this?"

"By some rocks close to Schemiel."

"Any marks on the dust?"

"Nothing new that I could see. The marks of the wreck's passage are filling in, and anything smaller would have smoothed out almost at once. You know how that stuff acts. It's like water." Carter added, "Would they have gone so close to the dust? Harmond was pretty cautious and Chagny never liked to take chances if he could help it."

The reason both had been picked. Koenig said, "If you're wondering why I didn't want you to land, it was for two reasons. One, I didn't want you ruining any tracks there might be; the other reason you know. I— What's the matter, Bailey?"

The Eagle yawed a little, steadied as Carter took over the controls, levelling the craft and lifting it. In the co-pilot's chair Bailey blinked and shook his head.

"Funny," he said. "I could have sworn we were over Schemiel."

"We are." Carter was curt. "What's the matter, Chad, can't you read instruments anymore?"

"I can read them," snapped Bailey, "if they register correctly. Ours must be all haywire. This can't be Schemiel."

"Don't be a fool, man!"

"All right." Bailey was stubborn. "If this is Schemiel, where is the wreck?"

It had vanished. All of it. Below lay nothing but the crater, the broken rim-wall, the dust and starlit stone. The twisted remnants of the pod and tracery— all had gone.

CHAPTER FIVE

Bergman said, "When faced with the incredible, first eliminate the impossible and then what is left, no matter how improbable, must be the answer."

"Occams Razor," said Koenig sourly. "Or something like it."

"Actually I think it is a quotation attributed to Sherlock Holmes," said Bergman mildly. "Not that it matters. The advice is still good."

Koenig rose from his chair and strode across the floor of his office. Beyond the partition, now closed, Main Mission hummed with its usual activity, but here was an oasis of seclusion that he could change at any time to become one with Moonbase.

"Victor, it is impossible that the wreckage could have vanished without cause."

"Agreed." Bergman, sitting, toyed with a slide rule. "There has to be a cause, but what? A natural volatisation? Could the effect of impact have triggered some ingrained chemical combination that resulted in an abrupt vapourisation of the substance?"

"You think it possible?"

"John, I hardly know what to think. The thing was

alien and therefore, by definition, beyond our experience. I suppose that such a change in apparently adamantine material is possible, but only remotely so. I'd put it in the order of things that could happen, but only because in a universe composed of an infinity of possibilities nothing is or can be impossible." Then, seeing Koenig's expression, he added, "I'm sorry. You aren't in the mood for philosophy."

"Not with two men dead, Victor."

"There is no doubt?"

"None." Koenig halted his pacing. "I knew that before I ordered the Eagle not to land. Helena had reported that their life-monitors had ceased to function. In any case, there isn't the remotest chance of their being alive after all this time."

For days the entire area around Schemiel had been searched inch by inch by teams of men roped together and guarded by others. Koenig had been among them and his reddened eyes and haggard features told of his fatigue.

"Nothing!" The fist of one hand slammed into the palm of the other. "No traces, no signs, nothing but rock and dust. Something must have caused that wreckage to vanish, and something must have killed those men." He added bitterly, "Aside from myself, of course, but if it hadn't been for me, they would still be alive."

"You mean if I hadn't persuaded you not to volatise the object," said Bergman. "If it hadn't been diverted those men would be alive now—is that what you're thinking?"

"Isn't it true?"

"Yes, it's true enough, John, but why blame yourself? I was responsible, not you. They were collecting seeds on my orders, not yours." Bergman looked at the rule in his hands and let it fall. It landed on the desk with a brittle clatter. "Blame," he said bitterly. "Always we must take the blame. But is it our fault if we are unable to see into the future? Must ignorance always carry the burden of guilt?"

"How can you deny it? You—" Koenig broke off, remembering how the man had lost his wife. Those with power must always carry the guilt—it was the price they paid for the authority they were given, but this was no time to open old wounds and to revive old pain. And Victor had not been to blame. Only in his mind could he consider himself guilty for the crash that had taken her and left him to mourn. In a more even tone he said, "What's happened is past. Recriminations serve no purpose. Two men are dead. I want to know who or what killed them, and I'm not interested in philosophical abstractions. I want facts. Facts!"

They were too few: the recorded transcript of their last communication, Carter's evidence, Bailey's statement of a movement he'd spotted or thought he'd spotted. The mysterious vanishing of the wreckage.

The incredible.

Remove the impossible and what was left? And how to decide what was impossible?

"Nothing came from space," said Bergman. "Even if it had been invisible and somehow lifted the wreckage, we would have spotted an energy nexus. So it has to be a local phenomenon."

"No Lunar disturbance was registered," said Koenig. "And if a fissure had opened to swallow the men and then closed and opened again to engulf the wreckage, there would have been traces. Eliminate that. Let's listen to that recording again."

It washed from the speakers, a sound now all too familiar by constant repetition, ghostly, somehow eerie, the words hopelessly distorted but carrying an unmistakable terror.

"We can't clear it," said Bergman as the recording came to an end. "I've been working on it together with others. It's impossible to eliminate the background noise and isolate the words. If we could we might be able to break and blend them into some recognisable pattern."

"Conclusion?"

"It wasn't just noise. If it was, we could achieve separation. The static, for want of a better term, was inherent in the broadcast. Those men must have been surrounded by an intensely powerful electro-magnetic field that built resonance currents into their radios."

"A field that had to originate somewhere." Koenig frowned. "The dust?"

"It does hamper radio transmission in a similar manner," admitted Bergman. "But it is usually not so intense. And the broadcast was distorted from the beginning, don't forget. If a man were falling, he'd have time to shout a few clear words, and certainly his companion would not have been affected—not unless both fell at exactly the same time."

"Not impossible, but highly improbable," said Koenig bitterly. "Victor, this is getting us nowhere. We're just speculating and making wild guesses. It isn't good enough. I've got to find out exactly what happened to those two men."

The men and the wreckage—there was no place for such mysteries on the Moon.

David Kano wasn't married to the computer, but even so, he took it to bed with him. A terminal had been installed in his room so that, even when relaxing, he was in close touch with the instrument that dominated his life.

Now, with its aid, he was solving a problem.

"More data will be needed before a correlation can be made and a conclusion delivered," said the machine. It had a soft and pleasing feminine voice, which he chose to use instead of the word-pictures thrown on a screen or the more customarily used read-outs. Each had their place, but for him the voice held a comfort.

A fantasy, as he would be the first to admit, but a harmless one. Warriors of all ages have named and personalised their weapons and steeds. Sportsmen did the same with their vehicles. Kano had done no more than they had. To think of the computer as a thing alive—well, who could say that it wasn't?

No one—if they wanted to retain his friendship.

Now he gave the necessary figures, reading them from the lists compiled by the technicians who had measured the wreck. Data that provided a topological nightmare in its series of complex curves and that would have kept a skilled mathematician busy for weeks to achieve the essential exactitude.

Even the computer took a little time—a few seconds longer than it took Kano to read the data.

He noted the answer.

More figures, this time relatively simple, the answer coming immediately. An equation, a mathematical exercise, figures that he correlated on his pad.

"Are you certain?"

"I fail to understand the question." The voice, in his imagination, held a certain chill. "I am incapable of error."

"Sorry." The incongruity of apologising to a machine never occurred to him. "I meant that there is no possibility of an alternative solution?"

"The conclusion I supplied, based on the figures you gave, is correct."

And unexpected. Kano checked his notations and thoughtfully pursed his lips. In his world two and two should always make a nice, neat, understandable four and, if the answer was different, then something somewhere was very wrong.

Lifting his commlock he activated the instrument and said to the operator, "Commander Koenig, please."

"He's engaged. Will you hold or try again later?"

"I'll hold."

Koenig had been talking to Reconnaissance, ordering Eagles to prepare for another search. As he lowered the commlock it hummed again and he looked at Kano's face.

"Yes?" He frowned at the answer. "Are you certain? Good. That's excellent. Yes. Yes, of course, come here immediately. I'm in my office." To Bergman he said, "We may have found something. Kano thinks so and I hope to God he's right. It could be the solution to the mystery."

It was based on an inconsistency as the technician explained when, minutes later, he joined the others in the large office. He sat at Koenig's invitation, clearing a space on the desk, pushing aside a litter of papers and empty coffee containers.

"I was running routine data through the computer," he said, "when something began to nag at me. You know how it is, Professor, something's wrong, you don't know what, but you'd stake your life that it's there. Well, with me it was like that. Something just didn't seem to make sense, so I did some digging."

"And found?"

"Something odd, Commander. First I had the computer find me the exact volume of the interior of the wreck. Then the exact volume of one of the seeds. From those figures it was simple to determine how many seeds could have been carried within the pod. Naturally I requested optimum packing arrangements."

"And so you discovered the probable number of seeds carried." Bergman nodded. "I'd run similar checks myself. The number, of course, is high."

"How high?" Koenig was sharp. "We didn't find all that many."

"Eighty-seven to be exact," said Bergman. "But many could have been scattered far beyond the region of the wreck, and some must have fallen into the dust. In fact, in light of the carrying capacity of the pod, they must have done so. With a more extensive search we shall find more."

"Perhaps not, Professor." Kano touched the papers he had brought with him. "In fact, the computer findings show they probably do not exist to be found."

"What?"

"I didn't stop at just determining the different volumes. I determined the mass of one of the seeds, then extrapolated what the total mass would be if the pod was filled to capacity." Kano paused, then added quietly, "I found a discrepancy. I had the computer check and re-check, but there is no doubt as to the figures. They show that the pod could not have been carrying a full load of seeds."

Koenig said, "You're certain as to that?"

"The figures prove it. If the pod had been filled, then its mass would have been far greater than what we know it was. Those seeds are heavy and there would have been a lot of them. To be precise, there would have been room for twenty-five thousand six hundred eighteen. Eighty-seven have been found and, even allowing for more yet to be discovered, there is a vast differential."

"And the mass?" Bergman looked up from his slide rule. "What is the differential between the actual and the assumed?" He pursed his lips as Kano gave the answer. "You aren't ignoring the surrounding tracery?"

"No. I've established a probable norm using the established system. The differential still exists." He repeated, this time with greater emphasis, "That pod could not have been filled with seeds."

Koenig stepped to the communications post, hit the switch and said, "Get me Nancy Coleman immediately." As he waited he said to Kano, "I'm not doubting you, David, but I have to be sure. Nancy? A question. In your experience do any seed pods exist that are only barely full?"

"Commander?"

He repeated the question, amplifying it with, "Do any such pods use some form of cushion-mechanism, wadding or something like that? Gas, even, or something that vanishes when the pod breaks open?" Impatience edged his voice as she hesitated. "Hurry, please, this is urgent."

"I was thinking, Commander. Botany covers a wide field and in nature almost anything is possible. Offhand I'd say the answer to your question is no. Nature as well as being versatile is also extremely conservative in the sense that nothing goes to waste. A pod carries a certain number of seeds and usually always the same number. Safety is achieved by lightness and adhesion. In some cases by a form of suspension, such as a normal, garden pea, which grows from a stem within the pod. Protection comes from the outer wrapping, such as Brazil nuts, which are found closely packed in a tough casing. And the coconut, despite its shell, carries a thick layer of fibre to cushion its impact with the ground. On the other hand—"

"So the answer is no," broke in Koenig.

"As far as my experience goes, Commander, that is correct."

"Thank you." Turning from the communications post, Koenig looked at the others. "Well?"

"There were no traces of any cushioning material within the pod," said Bergman. "And no signs of any form of adhesion or suspension of the seeds. Until now I had assumed they had been carried closely packed. David has shown that to have been impossible. Assuming the pod would not have been empty, only one conclusion is left."

Something had travelled inside.

Above Schemiel the Eagle hovered like a moth above a flame, veering a little, lifting to fall to lift again, tiny movements almost indiscernible to the unaided eye, but too much for Carter to tolerate.

"Give me the controls," he snapped to Bailey. "Take over the monitor."

The co-pilot obeyed, a dull flush staining his cheeks, knowing better than to complain at such a moment. He relaxed a little as Carter, startled, swore as the Eagle fought his control.

"What the hell? Chad, was this Eagle checked out?"

"One hundred percent operational, skipper."

"Then what's wrong? I can't keep it level and the stability's all shot to hell. Check the systems."

Bailey threw back a cover and made a rapid test of the automatic maintenance circuits.

"All functioning, skipper," he reported. "Some increase in the ion level, but nothing above tolerance."

Whose tolerance was a matter of opinion, but it wasn't Carter's. For him only perfection was good enough, and if the automatics couldn't supply it, then he'd do without them.

"Stand by for manual override." He moved a lever. "Manual engaged. I'm taking over, Paul."

Seated at his console in Main Mission, Paul Morrow shrugged.

"It's your decision, Alan, but keep that Eagle level. I want to take as accurate a reading as possible of the surface dust in Schemiel. What was wrong, anyway?"

"Electrical buildup in the guidance systems, which caused over-compensation. We seem to be picking up a charge from somewhere." He added grimly, "If it isn't that, then someone in maintenance will have some questions to answer and, if he can't do it to my satisfaction, Medical will have a new customer."

"You and whose army, Alan?"

"Just me. When my neck's at stake I don't need an army to back me up when talking to the crumb who skipped his job."

"If someone did skip it." Morrow was serious. "I think you know better than that. You'd better have Bailey run a separate, continual check on all potentials in the Eagle."

"Agreed." Carter nodded to his co-pilot. "Get with it, Chad, and if you've still got a burn, I apologise. It wasn't your fault, and I jumped too hard and too soon. Now let's get with it."

The Eagle dropped lower to hover just above the dust at a carefully determined point. Lower and its blast would catch the fine powder and send it swirling up and over the area. Too high and the inverse-square law would reduce any weak signal to a level impossible to distinguish against the normal background level of radioactive "noise." And it would be a weak signal; Koenig was sure of that.

He stood at the edge of the crater, other suited figures set at regular intervals in a wide arc to either side. All were roped to each other and all were armed with heavy-duty lasers. A second Eagle, grounded, stood well to the rear but ready to lift at a moment's warning. It, too, was armed with missiles primed and ready to go, its laser warmed, its crew on battle alert.

"Paul?"

"Nothing yet, Commander." Morrow's voice was clear over the radio. "Background radiation a little high, but general."

"That's to be expected, John," said Bergman from where he waited in Main Mission. "The wreck would have contaminated the ground when it touched. Its radioactive level was higher than Lunar normal."

"I know, Victor. Jamson!" A man lifted his arm at the end of the left-hand arc. "You're too close to the edge. Back off a little."

Koenig leaned back as the Eagle came towards him, turned, then made another crossing of the crater. Carter was handling it well, and if there was anything for his instruments to find, they would find it.

If anything was to be found at all.

Koenig looked back at the crater. The walls were peaked, jagged, fretted with fissure lines, most old, but some, especially those at close hand, new. The gap made by the wreck marred the rim-wall as a missing tooth marred an otherwise attractive mouth. The surface of the dust was barely marked now, the fine powder settling under the influence of the low gravity. Soon it would be the smooth expanse it had been before the alien visitor had crashed on the Moon.

The pod and what it must have contained.

Logic had determined that the alien pods must have

held more than seeds, and now the same logic pointed to where the passenger, whatever it was, must be hiding. Unless a master of perfect camouflage, the alien would be beneath the surface of the smooth dust, hiding like a fish in water, safely invisible to any normal search.

A lair from which it had risen to kill two men—to kill them and somehow dispose of their bodies. To later dispose of the debris of the pod.

But why?

And how?

Logic, I must use logic, thought Koenig grimly. The mental tool that could be used like a razor. Eliminate the impossible and what remained, no matter how improbable, must be the answer. But what could be more improbable than an unknown form of life that could both live in an airless void and kill and dispose of creatures that must be as alien to it as it was to them?

"Paul?"

"Still no positive readings, Commander."

"Why not fire into the crater?" said a man. "If anything's there, it'll stir it up."

A reaction he might not enjoy. Koenig remembered the volume of the interior of the pod; the thing that had occupied it could have the bulk of an Eagle. Yet it was a way to solve the impasse—obviously they couldn't stand guard forever.

"Alan!"

"Commander?"

"Lift and fire at the far side of the crater. Use your laser, and remember, we're standing close."

"I'll watch it," promised the pilot. "I'll give a ten-second preliminary warning, then a five-second . . ." His voice blurred. ". . . on cue. Understood?"

"No!" In Main Mission Paul Morrow was anxious. "I didn't get that. Please repeat. Understood? Please repeat. Your transmission was . . ."

Koenig winced as a rush of grinding static came from his radio. Through his face-plate he could see others with hands lifted to their helmets, one running in small circles as if unable to stand the jarring noise. It grew, drowned what seemed to be words, caused his own to bounce back and add to the din.

"Retreat!" he yelled. "Back off, all of you! Back off! Eagle Two! Lift! Lift and rescue!"

An order they couldn't have heard and, not hearing, couldn't obey. Koenig waved his arms, gesturing, turning to face the crater while busy with his emergency semaphoring.

And then he saw it.

And froze.

It was a thing from nightmare—blurred, huge, rising from the centre of the crater, dust rising from flailing appendages, the starlight gleaming from something that looked like polished marble, striated, ebon mixed with pearl.

An opening that gaped.

Above, the Eagle came driving down, laser flaring, a beam of light so intense that it hurt the eyes and left dancing after-images, followed by a temporary blindness as the visual purple in the eyes was bleached from the rods and cones.

Blinded, Koenig stumbled and fell, remembering what he had seen in the glare; the small figure swept from its feet, lifted, spinning as it dropped into its gaping mouth. How many others would follow? Men crushed and broken, suits torn, air lost, delicate tissues ruptured beneath the strain of explosive decompression.

What screams would he be hearing if there were no static?

His knees jarred against stone and he toppled to roll and catch his gloved hands on a shard of rock. Blinking, cursing the retinal images that painted his vision with lances of red and orange, yellow and amber, he stared towards the crater. It held a swirling mass of dust, powder flung high and hovering before it fell, almost motionless in the airless void. Then, in the dust, something moved and rock splintered inches before his face.

Shards dashed against his face-plate, starring the transparency, rendering it opaque even as it fractured the tough material.

To the rushing blur of electronic noise was added another—that of the hiss of escaping air.

Koenig was dying, and he knew it. Weakened internal pressure would blow out the entire face-plate to expose his face to the emptiness of space. For a moment he would see it, feel the escaping air gush from his lungs; then his eyes would become immediately dehydrated, his blood would foam and his lungs would shred as they yielded to internal stress.

His hands slapped at the emergency pouch on his thigh, found a cover-seal, ripped it free and lifted it to slap it over the fractured face-plate. Another followed, a third, more following as he added to the protection, praying that the adhesive would hold, that the seals would cover an area for which they had never been designed, that luck, which had kept him alive so far, would not desert him now.

He was still praying when another blow slammed against the rear of his helmet and threw him into oblivion.

CHAPTER SIX

Koenig was dead and in hell and someone was calling his name. "John! John Koenig! Commander!"

To move was to make too great an effort, and the reality waiting was something he could do without.

"John! John, please!"

Helena? But what would an angel be doing in the devil's domain? With an effort Koenig opened his eyes and stared at a face wreathed with golden hair, at eyes that held anxiety, at a mouth that smiled.

"Good, you've decided to make the effort. I wondered how long it would be."

Words that were a mask to cover trepidation; an attitude he recognised for being what it was. A form of self-defence that provided a barrier against a betrayal of emotion.

He said flatly, "I expected to die."

"You almost did." Helena checked the monitor-case over his chest, uncoupled it and swung it aside. "John, if you've ever considered yourself unlucky, now is the time to change your mind. You should be dead. The others—" She broke off, biting her lip, then said again, "You were lucky."

68

"And the others weren't." It wasn't a question. "How many?"

"Eight. Six dead."

Eight from a dozen; three others had survived aside from himself—if the remaining two should live.

"One has a chance," said Helena when he asked the question. "Both legs broken and some ribs, extensive bruising and a bad case of concussion. The other lost air and had massive internal hemorrhaging. I've put him in intensive care."

"Name?"

"Peter Lodge."

Koenig closed his eyes, remembering a young, intense face, a pair of burning blue eyes, hair that had graced a high, smooth forehead. A technician with a brain and application above normal.

"He has a chance, John," said Helena quietly. "Not much of a chance, but at least he isn't dead."

She didn't add "not yet," but she didn't have to. Koenig did it for her—mentally, but he did it just the same.

"And me?"

"Bruises and mild concussion. You managed to seal your helmet in time and the blow that knocked you out flattened you with your face-plate in the dust. It provided a barrier against the internal pressure. Someone on Eagle Two had sense enough to realise something was wrong. They lifted and came to the rescue while Alan did his best to distract whatever it was you found in the crater. What was it, John?"

"Didn't he tell you?"

"I've been busy and so has he. Victor ordered a constant watch maintained over Schemiel with Eagles set close for instant action if needed." Pausing, she said again, "What was it, John?"

"A thing. A nightmare."

"Tell me. I insist!"

Looking at her he realised it was no idle question, no desire to pander to curiosity. The physician was foremost, and with the physician was the psychiatrist, and with them both the neurosurgeon and the—he frowned, trying to remember all her achievements, her degrees.

"John?"

"Ask the others."

"I did; they weren't any help. Dust rose and, in it something moved. Some force broke the rope attaching them to the others, and that same force threw them back over the rim-wall."

"Too bad," he said, "that they can't tell you, I mean."

"I'm not just being curious, John," she said quietly. "You saw something out there that almost killed you, but it did more than just knock you unconscious. You were raving when they brought you in. Screaming, fighting, like a man in delirium, a man who had seen something that had made him want to run, to hide. We had to straighten you from the foetal position. And in case you think you're normal now, you're not. I've pumped you full of drugs—nothing to worry about, just a heavy dose of tranquillizers with a mild depressant. Now, John, look at me and tell me what you saw—if you dare."

A challenge he was reluctant to meet, but one which, he knew, she would not let him avoid. He had to remember—had to!

Closing his eyes, he was back on the rim-wall of Schemiel, turning to watch the pluming dust, hearing the grating noise from the radio, seeing the thing that lifted and . . . and . . .

"Steady, John!" He felt the touch of something cool on his forehead, and opening his eyes, he saw Helena's face close to his own, her eyes misted with more than anxiety.

"You're safe now," she said soothingly. "Quite safe."

He said wonderingly, "I saw it, Helena. I'm sure I saw it, and yet I can't describe it. I don't even want to think about it. Each time I attempt to visualize the thing, something happens. The images blur and I get afraid. I want to run, and at the same time I want to hide, to drop and curl up into a ball, to bury my head in my arms and close out the world. Why?"

She said obliquely, "Was it large, John? One of the others said he caught a glimpse of what he thought of as a whale."

"Yes, it was big."

"And had a mouth?"

"A maw—yes, I guess you could call it a mouth."

"And things like arms? Tentacles, perhaps?"

Or pincers or claws or scrabbling limbs or suckers or ropes or furry spines or . . .

"All right, John." He heard the soft hiss of a hypodermic syringe as it blasted drugs into his bloodstream. His throat was sore and he had a dim memory of someone screaming. Himself? Had he screamed? Helena nodded when he asked. "You went into the initial stages of hysterical withdrawal. You'll be all right now."

"No!" He forced himself to sit upright on the bed. The lights bore little halos—miniature rainbows like those he had seen around the stars when he had first examined the heavens with a cheap telescope. The result of using non-achromatic lenses and which had made his initial investigations almost useless. Now he guessed they were a by-product of the drugs he'd been given. "Don't humour me, Helena. I've got to know— I saw that thing, so why can't I remember it?"

"Perhaps because you don't want to go insane. Look at it this way, John, you saw something so alien that you couldn't fit it into any recognisable pattern. At the same time you were faced with imminent death. On the subconscious level the mind has the tendency to lump such things together. You saw something alien, and you were faced with death; therefore, the alien thing equates with personal extinction. So each time you try to remember it in any detail, the subconscious—anticipating the other part of the equation, the realisation of death—rebels. It throws you into amnesiac shock. Basically, it is a primitive defence mechanism to ensure continued survival."

Then, before he could comment, she added, "Of course, there could be another reason."

"Such as?"

"The brain is as much an electrically motivated instrument as, say, a radio. We know that the proximity of the thing led to a breakdown in communications. Even the guidance systems of Alan's Eagle were affected. You were very close to the thing, John. It's possible that your brain was affected by its electronic field. The thing could even generate it as a form of protection. Its victims—for want of a better word—would be disorganised, deranged and frozen to form easy prey. Should they manage to escape, then the protection would continue. They would be unable to remember with any clarity what they had seen or what had happened. You're not an animal, and so you can and do—up to a degree."

He said, "Photographs. Alan must have been monitoring the area."

Sandra Benes set up the screen, taking time to say, "We're all glad you made it, Commander, very glad."

"Thank you."

"A nice girl," said Bergman as she left and the doors separating the office from Main Mission slid shut. "Usually unemotional, which makes her eminently suited to her position, but I'd swear she was crying when he reported that he thought you'd been killed."

Koenig said, "Let's get on with it, Victor. You've maintained the surveillance?"

"Pending your decision, yes." Bergman looked up from the projector. "I thought it best to take no positive action until you'd recovered."

Or died, in which case Bergman would have taken over Alpha until such time as a new commander had been decided upon.

"Ready, John?" Then, as Koenig nodded, Bergman switched on the projector. "This is from direct film," he explained as the screen filled with light and colour.

"The relayed transmission was good to begin with, then became useless as interference caused massive distortion. Alan is making his initial survey."

Images flowed over the screen, the crater of Schemiel, the rim-wall, the tiny figures of suited men. Koenig placed himself, eyes moving from one to the other; men now dead and alive only in the records.

Another pass, a third, a little lower this time and then—

"This is when the interference ruined transmission," said Bergman. "Now watch!"

Dust spun within the bowl of the crater, flowing like water, pouring from the mound of something that rose to bulk, gigantic against the tiny figures of men. A thing that swirls, thrashes, dust rising from all sides to cast a cloud of slowly moving particles, an umbrella that shielded what lay below.

The scene froze as Bergman touched a switch.

"This is the best view we were able to obtain," he explained. "Later the dust-cloud thickens. But it is obvious the thing is large. It also seems to be invulnerable to laser-fire—Alan swears he scored a direct hit. The ebon and pearl striations seem to be a protective covering and the colours could be a form of protective mimicry. There also seems to be evidence of a mouth and appendages of some kind." He touched the screen with a finger. "Here, here and here, John. You see?"

"Yes." Koenig was sweating and there was a faint ringing in his ears. "How often did Alan fire?"

"Twice. Both times with no apparent effect." Bergman started the projector and rewound the spool. "The rest is much the same. Alan stayed on guard while the other Eagle effected the rescue."

"Did he maintain watch over the area?"

"From a high altitude, yes. There was no point in taking chances. The dust had spread to cover the entire area, so he could see nothing, and I didn't want to risk losing an eagle."

A wise decision. Koenig said, "What do you make of it, Victor?"

"The creature?" Bergman became thoughtful. "It's alien, of course, which means it could be totally beyond our terms of reference, but working on the basis of observed data, we know, or can fairly assume, certain aspects of its nature. For one thing, it is an extremely tough life-form. It survived the blast of the atomic missile that diverted the pod. It survived the shock of the crash and it didn't appear to be hurt by a laser blast, which would have fused an Eagle."

A living thing that needed no air to survive, which could withstand high temperature differentials and generate a protective electronic-distortion field. But all things needed to eat in order to live. Food that could be turned into energy or energy taken direct.

Bergman nodded when he mentioned it.

"It's barely feasible, John, and certainly the evidence leads in that direction. We have no way of knowing how long it was within the pod, but I think it is safe to assume that it was in a dormant condition. The initial laser-blast may have awakened it, or the later atomic rain from the diverting missile may have triggered it off. Those traceries around the pod could also have been energy collectors. Then the crash and the splitting open of the pod. Schemiel would have offered an immediate hiding place, a close protection."

"From what?"

"From any hostile observer. A predator, perhaps, or excessive radiation. How can we tell what the conditions are on its home world? In any case, it is the natural instinct of any newborn life to seek protection."

"And to kill?"

"To eat, John," corrected Bergman. "Those men simply happened to be there."

"And the debris of the pod?"

"Food." Bergman was emphatic. "Many of our own insects follow the same pattern. Once they emerge from their cocoons, the first thing they do is to eat it. It's a readily available supply of protein."

"Eat it!? Victor, do you realise that not even a laser could touch that pod, that only a diamond wheel managed to cut into it?"

"I know, John, but there is no other rational explanation. The creature must have pulled the debris into the crater while we were getting ready a search party. A missed opportunity," he added. "If an Eagle had been monitoring, we could have gotten decent photographs of it."

His voice held the regret of a frustrated scientist. Koenig said, "Hindsight, Victor. We always know what *should* have been done. At the time we had no idea anything could live out there."

"But there it is, John, and think of what it must be like, the things it could teach us. A living creature with the ability to live in the void. It seems incredible. How does it manage its energy exchange? How to turn rocks and minerals into sustenance? How long could it survive without air or heat? Thinking of it reminds me of viruses—they, too, can live in hostile environments, remaining dormant until triggered into activity. A virus, John. There are analogies."

Koenig said flatly, "It must be destroyed."

Had the first man who'd ever seen a horse had the same reaction? Bergman pondered the question as he later stood with Koenig in Main Mission. The urge to kill was strong in the human race. The determination to eliminate the unknown by emotionally dictated destruction. To survive at no matter what cost.

How many tribes had been wiped out in the early days because they had been strangers venturing into another's territory? How many latent geniuses had been destroyed because they had appeared a little different to the accepted norm?

"John, isn't there some other way? Do you have to destroy it?"

"You have an alternative?"

"We could monitor the area, trap it in some way. Confine it so as to make tests and studies. It's something new, John. It could even be intelligent. Why kill what you can't understand?"

"There are eight men dead, Victor."

"An accident."

"Maybe."

"How could it be intentional? The thing was following an instinctive pattern of survival. It might even be in confusion and reacting on a basic primitive level. We don't know; that's the whole point. We simply don't know. Why must we be afraid of it just because it's alien?"

Alien and dangerous in a way he couldn't begin to appreciate.

Patiently Koenig explained, ending with, "That thing could never be taken alive. And even if it could, how would we hold it? We haven't the facilities to build and guard a cage. And the risk is too great."

"But need we be in so much of a hurry?"

"Victor, you—" Koenig snatched at his commlock as it hummed. "Helena?" His face tightened as she spoke. "I see. Yes, do what you can. Tell her I'm sorry, Helena, but . . . well, just tell her."

As he clipped the instrument to his belt, Koenig said, "Peter Lodge just died, Victor. His girl was with him and tried to commit suicide. If Helena hadn't been there, the death total caused by that thing out there would be ten, not nine. I don't want that total to get larger. Paul, are the Eagles set?"

"All ready, Commander." Morrow was at the console. "Alan will drop the bomb when you give the word."

"Kano?"

"Computer has checked all figures. The shock wave will be well within acceptable limits."

"Sandra, maintain continual monitoring." Koenig drew in his breath. "All right, Paul. Give the order."

On the main screen the drifting shapes of the Eagles reminded him of a swarm of fireflies, their command modules giving them an insect-like appearance, an impression heightened by the wink of starlight from rounded surfaces, the yellow gleam of light from the eye-like direct vision ports. They hung in a wide circle around Schemiel, watching, waiting. One, higher than the rest, hovered above the crater itself.

Compared to the others it was a skeleton, the passenger module removed and a jury-rigged assembly in its place. A thing of wires and drums and grabs that held the bulk of a carefully designed bomb.

"Eagle One," said Morrow. "Eagle One."

"Eagle One. I copy."

"Commence operation. I repeat. Commence operation."

The grabs dropped, the wire unreeling from its drum, the bomb hanging like a mass of lead from the installation. It fell, slowed, fell again as Carter manipulated the Eagle and Bailey the bomb controls.

He said, "Why go to all this trouble, skipper? We could have blasted the crater with missiles. We don't need to pussyfoot around with this special bomb."

"You heard the briefing," said Carter. "Fired missiles would have caused too much surface damage and pasted the area with radioactives. This way we put one bomb right down where we need it and, when detonated, the walls of the crater itself will act as blast-guides. If the figures are right, the blast will shoot all the debris into space."

"Like a shotgun." Bailey grinned as he let out more wire. "My great-great-great-grandpappy would have been good at this. He could load and fire a musket within thirty seconds. That's what we're doing, really, isn't it—loading a kind of musket to blow whatever is in that crater to hell and gone?" His tone changed. "Check three feet from surface."

"Check." Carter looked at his instruments and reported to Main Mission. "No sign of control aberration. All systems optimum. Proceed?"

"Proceed."

Bailey said, "Well, here goes!"

Beneath them was an atomic bomb suspended from a cable. If something should make it detonate before they were clear, then he, Carter and the entire Eagle would be turned into an incandescent cloud. And no one could be certain that the thing that had distorted radio transmission wouldn't also trigger the fuse of the bomb.

"Ready to release," said Bailey. He was sweating. "Bomb approximately one foot beneath dust."

And therefore right on target.

"Release!" Carter waited, counting seconds. At three he fed power to the drive and sent the Eagle darting away from the area above Schemiel. "Paul? Bomb released and on its way. Keep your fingers crossed."

And pray if that was your inclination. Pray that the mathematicians had been right, that the explosion would be contained, that the thing it was intended to destroy would become a column of expanding vapour blasting from the Moon.

Alpha ejecting an unwanted visitor.

One that had killed.

"Twenty-nine," said Bailey. "Thirty, thirty-one, thirty-two, thirty-three— What's keeping it?"

Already it was five seconds late according to his count, but Carter used a more efficient means of measuring the passage of time.

"Relax, Chad. You're counting too fast. There's two seconds to go as yet. You—" He broke off as a lamp flashed on the panel before him. "There she goes!"

At first there was nothing. Matter, sunken deep beneath the dust, had impacted, blossomed into violent expansion, atomic fragments shattering, releasing the titanic energy they contained. A pause that was but the merest flicker, and then the released energies took the dust and fused some and lifted some and threw the whole mass up and out in a ravening blast of livid blue-white flame.

A manmade volcano that left nothing behind it but

a fused hole—the crater of Schemiel swept clean as if with a broom and devoid of any trace of dust, of loose stone, of debris of any kind.

And empty of alien life.

CHAPTER SEVEN

Nancy Coleman took the spoonful of soil, placed it into a test tube, added liquid and gave the whole thing a vigorous shaking. Carefully labelling the container of muddy water, she set it aside in a rack with others. Later they would be tested, but she was confident of what the results would be. The acidity, mineral content, humus and nitrogen-factor were all favourable, as previous tests had shown, and the check was only a part of the system she had devised for routine maintenance.

"Everything all right, Nancy?" Constance Boswell entered the office. Her hands were grimy and a smudge of dirt on one cheek gave her a gamin-like appearance. Crossing to the faucet, she washed her hands. "I've been checking the experimental area. Nothing as yet, and maybe there never will be, but it's exciting."

"Different from the hydroponic farms?"

"This is the real thing," said Connie. "The other is the scientific production of edible vegetable matter in a controlled environment. All right, so the stuff being grown tastes and looks exactly the same, in some cases even better, but to me there's something missing."

The sun warm on back and shoulders, the feel of dirt beneath the fingers, the smell of the loam, the sense of belonging to the land. Nancy Coleman could understand all that so well. Leaning back in her chair, she half-closed her eyes, remembering when she had been a girl, little more than a child, running through fields thick with ripening grain, weeding, watching as life burst from the soil to strive for a place in the sun.

A time that had passed all too quickly, and then came the studies, the endless learning, the finding of her profession. It had been natural to turn to botany, natural to experiment with hybrids and to stimulate vegetable germ plasm with selected radioactivity.

Her development of a new strain of wheat had won her worldwide recognition as being at the summit of her profession. Moonbase Alpha had offered her the chance to pursue her experiments using accelerated techniques based on a low-gravity environment. Her Luna Orchid had taken the botanical world by storm. If things had progressed as anticipated, she would have been able to retire both rich and famous to the small estate she had purchased in the Lesser Antilles.

At times she wondered what had happened to it.

She said, opening her eyes, "You're a natural-born farmer, Connie. That's why you don't wear gloves when working with the soil—you like to feel it against your skin. And don't forget to wash your face."

"Face?"

"You've got dirt on your left cheek." Nancy smiled as the girl removed the dirt. Young, with a subtle but disturbing beauty, the girl would have to be careful if she wasn't to break hearts. "Any news of Edward?"

"He proposed last night."

"And?"

"I said that I'd think it over." Connie threw aside the towel. "Anything new in Eden?"

The name that Rural Area One had become known by. Eden, a new world, a small one as yet, but it could grow. Her world, thought Nancy Coleman, a little smugly. One in which she was in charge. A good exchange for the estate she had lost.

Rising, she stepped to the door of the office and outside to stand in the light of the artificial sun. The cavern still held a spartan bleakness, but soon all that would change. Once the soil had been finally balanced, seeds would be sown, the loam turning green with new life, the air taking to itself the scent of growing things. We could have a wind machine, she thought, something to provide a gentle breeze that would rustle the leaves and add to the illusion already created. A sound to blend with that of the fountain.

She moved towards it, her stride lengthening as she recognised the figure of Bergman stooping over a plot of dirt in a far corner.

"Anything as yet, Professor?"

"What? I—" He smiled and brushed soil from his hands. "Nancy, I didn't hear you. No, nothing as yet, as far as I can determine."

"Let me take a look."

Stooping, she uncovered one of the seeds and examined it. The surface looked as she remembered, the whorls perhaps a little less distinct, the diffusion of light not so pronounced. Lifting it, she held it to her cheek. Life, any form of life, was a manifestation of energy and change—both producing heat. With a seed so large it was barely possible she could distinguish a temperature rise. A test that failed. The skin remained as she remembered.

"Nothing, Professor, but in botany you have to be patient. Do you know how long it took me to develop W-725?"

"Fifteen years," he said. "And you ran over seven hundred tests on various strains of wheat. Even then you were lucky—the project could have lasted an entire lifetime."

"At times I think it did." She hefted the seed. "Do you want me to examine this for any signs of germination or should I just leave it in the ground?"

"Leave it—I don't want to take the chance of losing the only one that may grow."

"If it can, it will," she promised.

"Perhaps." Bergman wasn't as confident. "How do we know if the environment is right? It could be too warm or too wet, too cold or too dry. The loam may lack essential elements, or maybe it needs a stimulus I haven't given it."

And maybe it wasn't a seed at all. Something Koenig mentioned when he met Bergman after he'd left the cavern.

He said without preamble, "Victor, it would be best for us to dispose of those seeds."

"Dispose of them?" Bergman was incredulous. "Destroy them? John, you can't be serious."

"I'm serious," said Koenig grimly. "We've taken something alien into Moonbase and we have no idea as to its potential danger. It's associated with that creature we destroyed, and what do we really know about that?"

They were in Bergman's quarters and, before answering, he moved to adjust a framed certificate hanging against a wall. It was one given to him for his work in protecting a form of life threatened with extinction.

Recognising the tension betrayed by the set of the man's shoulders, the symbolism of touching the certificate, Koenig said quietly, "I'm being rational about this, Victor. My first concern is and must be the safety of Alpha. Nine men are dead and I don't want to add to their number. So, on calculation—"

"You choose to destroy rather than to understand." Bergman turned. "I'm going to fight you on this, John. I can appreciate your concern, but as yet you've not given me one reason why I should agree with your decision. You've not given a reason for your fears."

"I haven't made a decision," reminded Koenig. "If I had, Victor, believe me, we wouldn't be discussing the matter as we are now. I said it would be best for us to dispose of those seeds, and now I'll tell you why. They came in the pod that carried the alien creature, right?"

"Yes, John."

"So how did it get into it? Was it a cocoon spun for protection while the thing underwent a metamorphosis? In that case, those spheres we found can't be seeds. Was it a parasite living in the pod and feeding off of it? If so, there is still a doubt."

"John?"

"You're overlooking the obvious, Victor. You want those things to be seeds so much that you can't recognise the alternatives. As I see it, those spheres could be either of three things. If that creature belonged in the pod, they could be droppings. If it was a parasite that had somehow managed to enter the pod and then to feed on its interior as it grew, then they could be seeds. They could have been like those of a watermelon, resting imbedded in the pulp. Those possibilities don't worry me. The third one does."

Bergman said slowly, "John, I think you're wrong, but I know what you're getting at. You think those spheres could be—"

"Eggs, Victor," said Koenig harshly. "You could have planted a nest of serpents in Eden!"

Doctor Mathias dropped a slim sheaf of papers to the desk and, leaning against it with the easy casualness of long familiarity, said, "We'll have to make a decision soon, Doctor. Lynne Saffery can't be kept under constant sedation for much longer."

"I know, Bob."

"Already she is showing traces of fluid accumulation in both lungs, and her muscle tone shows signs of deterioration." He tapped the papers with the tip of a brown finger. "I've run a series of general physical checks and, unless she get's up and around soon, we could have complications."

Too many and too soon. Helena stared at the papers, frowning as she read the data, facts and figures that led to an inescapable conclusion.

She said thoughtfully, "This doesn't make sense, Bob. She hasn't been bedridden long enough for all this deterioration. Psychosomatic?"

"A possibility," he admitted. "But if so, then the circumstances are new to me. A girl, apparently insane, who has created her own deterioration by mental directives. I don't like it, Doctor."

"Neither do I." Helena triggered her commlock. "John? I'm going to attempt to revive Lynne Saffery. I thought you might be interested. Why?" She smiled at his question. "Well, she did try to eat you, John— or have you forgotten?"

The sore spot on his throat would have reminded him if he had. He touched it as he made his way to Medical Centre, the skin torn by snapping teeth, the wound healing beneath a scrap of transparent plastic. How long ago now? Days? A week? So much had happened since the girl had held him locked in her arms.

He paused as a squad of men moved along the corridor. Technicians on their way to the exterior to be suited and then lowered into nearby fissures, there to check if any threatening damage had been caused by the recent atomic blast.

A precaution and a part of normal maintenance procedure, but to ignore or forget it was to invite disaster. On the Moon eternal vigilance was the price of survival.

"John!" Helena smiled as Koenig entered Medical. "We're just about to begin."

"Is she cured?"

"We don't know." She anticipated his next question. "We can't leave her, John. I'm aware that natural sleep is the best healer there is, but we've kept her under sedation too long as it is. There are odd and disturbing complications. No girl as young as she is and in such good physical condition should display her symptoms."

He said, "Could they be a by-product of what caused her illness in the first place?"

"You're thinking of the possibility of a virus infection?" She shook her head as he nodded. "No, John, we've eliminated all possibility of danger from that source. If we had found something, it would have been easy to decide the cause of her breakdown; as it is, we can only guess and hope that she has made a natural recovery." She glanced to where Mathias stood beside the bed. "Ready, Bob?"

"When you give the word, Doctor."

"Go ahead."

The encephalogram, Koenig noticed, had been connected and he studied the pattern of wavy lines as Mathias injected the stimulant. They flickered, steadied, flickered again.

"Normal," commented Helena from where she stood at his side. "See how the pattern changes as she begins to regain consciousness? Now we have to hope that the previous distortion doesn't appear."

"And if it doesn't?"

"We can hope for a cure. At least her mental condition will be as it should be. That alien pattern—" she drew in her breath as the screen flared to a jumble of lines, then released it as it steadied again. "Thank God for that. Bob?"

"She's waking up." Mathias stepped back, the hypodermic syringe ready. "If she goes crazy, I'll have to sedate her again."

"On my order only." Helena stooped over the bed. "Lynne! Lynne, my dear, wake up! Wake up, Lynne!"

The girl turned and smiled and opened her eyes.

"Doctor! What a wonderful rest I've had. Did I fall asleep? I'm sorry. I didn't mean to spoil the test. Did I spoil it?"

"No," said Helena quickly. "How do you feel?"

"Relaxed." The girl stretched out like a cat as she lay supine on the bed, arms uplifted, the muscles of her thighs clear beneath the skin, breasts prominent against the cage of her ribs.

Koenig said dryly, "Not hungry?"

"No . . . well, a little," she amended. "And that's odd; I ate just before reporting for the test session."

Days ago now—and she remembered nothing of what had happened. Koenig met Helena's eyes and she answered the jerk of his head. Standing at the far side of the ward, he said quietly, "Would you say she is cured?"

"No."

"Her mind—"

"Seems clear enough at the moment," she interrupted, "but don't forget the amnesia. That isn't normal to begin with. And I can't understand how her encephalogram became so distorted. Hunger," she mused. "Bob said the pattern reminded him of a hunger line he'd once seen. And she tried to eat you, John. Given the chance, she would have torn out your throat. But why? Why? What made her do it?"

From where he stood beyond the head of the bed, Mathias said sharply, "Dr Russell! Please!"

They looked at an animal.

The contrast was too great, the change too revolting and Koenig felt his stomach contract as he looked at what moments before had been a young and lovely girl.

The creature was still a female and still young, but there the similarity ended. Lynne Saffery was no longer lovely and, he thought, no longer human.

"The encephalograph," said Helena. "Look at the screen!"

It writhed with the hatefully familiar jumble of lines he had seen before.

As her voice carried a hatefully familiar whine.

"Food! I need food! I must have food! Feed me! Feed me!"

"Doctor?" Mathias lifted his hypodermic syringe.

"No." Helena shook her head. "Not yet. John, help me to restrain her."

"No!" He looked at the girl. She was writhing on the bed in a peculiarly constricted motion, ripples running from head to foot as she inched along the couch.

"Why don't you get her something to eat?" he suggested. "Feed her as she asks."

"Assuage her longing?" Mathias looked thoughtful. "She doesn't seem to be as violent as before, Doctor. It could be that the commander has a point. And if she will eat naturally, it will help to bolster her constitution."

She ate like the animal she had become, grabbing food and thrusting it into her mouth regardless of mixed textures and flavours, unheeding of the scraps that fell from her hands and mouth to spatter her garment. A day's rations, two, and still she wanted more.

Even when restrained, she writhed and mewed and slavered, chewing at the pillow, the sheets, biting her lips until blood ran down her chin. Only when drugs had been injected into her bloodstream did she finally relax to fall into an artificial sleep.

"Food," said Koenig. "She seems to be obsessed with the desire to eat. Is there a disease that can cause such a condition?"

"A few, but they are rare and she has none of them." Helena was definite. "More common is the psychological desire that drives people to overeat—boredom, emotional instability, ingrained habit patterns, things like that. Again, as far as I can tell, Lynne has no problem of that nature."

Koenig looked at where she lay, knees updrawn, her face almost buried in the pillow. Thoughtfully he touched the dressing over the small wound.

Coincidence?

"Helena, when Lynne bit me, did you make a note of the time?"

"I did, Commander," said Mathias. "I had to sedate her, remember? And a note is always made of the time of any injection." He lifted the clipboard from the end of the bed. "Here it is. See?"

"And the initial distortion of her brain wave pattern? You have that, too?"

"Naturally."

Helena said, "What's on your mind, John? What bearing could this have on her condition?"

"Maybe none, but it needs to be checked out. Bob, get on to Kano. Give him all times and durations you have of the progression of Lynne's trouble. Have him check them against anything recorded in the computer. Anything at all. I don't care if a man burped in the dining hall at the time I was bitten—I want to know about it. Have him find correlations."

"You've thought of something," said Helena as the doctor moved over to the communications post. "An association of some kind. What is it, John?"

"Madness, perhaps." Again he touched his throat. "When you first sedated Lynne you were running experiments in telepathy, right?"

"In extrasensory perception," she corrected. "I was trying to narrow the field to determine in which area her talent was to be found. I'd eliminated clairvoyance and precognition."

"Which left telepathy?"

"It had to be that. I arrived at the conclusion that Lynne Saffery, in order to gain the high scores she did on the test cards, had to be reading my mind. I intended to enhance her sensitivity by hypnotic suggestion and see if her performance could be improved. Theoretically she could have achieved a one-hundred-percent success rate each and every time once she managed to handle her talent. Other advantages are obvious. But you gave the Yellow Alert and ended the experiment."

Koenig glanced at the bed, at the slim figure lying on the mattress, remembering his own fears, the sickness that had overwhelmed him when trying to remember details of the alien visitor. Remembering, too, the distortion of her brain wave pattern, her ravening hunger.

It all fitted, but he hoped he was wrong.

A hope that died as Mathias returned with the data from Main Mission.

"Kano ran the problem through the computer and

came up with certain related incidents. These he feels are the most appropriate and the only ones that fall into a common pattern." The doctor glanced at his papers. "According to the computer, Lynne's brain wave pattern showed an abrupt and violent distortion a few seconds after the atomic missile used to divert the pod was detonated. The distortion continued in varying intensity until, at the time the pod landed, there is an abrupt enhancing of the alien characteristics."

Something jarred to full awareness by the impact of the nuclear blast. Something shocked by the force of the crash when the pod had split and a new and hostile environment had to be faced.

"And when I was bitten?"

"That coincides with the time when the first two men died." Mathias looked up from his papers. "Commander, I can't believe it. It's incredible!"

"Telepathy," whispered Helena. "It has to be that. Somehow a mental link was established between Lynne and that creature from space. She was receiving the echoes of its mind. Its hunger drove her. Its ferocity made her act like a savage animal. Its domination even affected her basic metabolism. But, John, the thing was destroyed!"

Koenig said bitterly, "Was it?"

CHAPTER EIGHT

"Alive?" Bergman shook his head, baffled. "But how? Nothing can withstand the fury of an atomic explosion, and the bomb we detonated swept Schemiel clean. The rock was fused, unbroken. The dust and whatever else the crater contained were blasted into space in a column of incandescent vapour. No creature, no matter how alien, could have survived."

"An atomic blast, no."

"Then how—"

"Protective mimicry." Koenig was savage. A small depiction of one of the first interplanetary rocket probes toppled and fell as his hand slammed hard on the surface of his desk. "You mentioned it yourself, Victor—that pearl and ebon striation you spotted on the photograph. And it had time to leave the crater, don't forget. After the rescue when Alan was hovering on guard and the other Eagle collected the injured and dead. Dust, you said, thick enough to cover the entire area—thick enough to cover movement, too." His hand slapped at a button. "Sandra. Get me photographs of Schemiel taken before we blasted it, some

just after and some taken recently. If you haven't any
on file, send out to get them."

"We have them, Commander." Her face, on the
screen, was bland. "The ones taken after the detona-
tion are not very good. The dust—"

"I know about the dust. Send them into my office.
No, never mind, I'll come out."

The doors opened as he aimed and activated his
commlock and Koenig swept into Main Mission.
Morrow glanced curiously at him from his position at
the console, an expression matched by Kano and
Benes herself. She said, "On the auxilliary screens,
Commander. You want me to run a comparison?"

"Yes. Commence immediately."

Three screens sprang to life, the one in the centre
showing a blur of dust. It moved as he watched and he
knew it was the record that had been taken by the
hovering Eagle.

"As you see, John, it hides all detail," commented
Bergman.

"And provides cover."

"Yes."

A blanket beneath which anything could be hiding.
Koenig turned to the first screen, studied it, then
moved to the third.

"Sandra, how recent is the last photograph?" He
frowned at the answer. "Flash me ones taken earlier."

"They'll come up as the dust cloud settles, Commander." The screen blurred as she spun the record,
then settled to show thinning wisps. "Better?"

"Yes." Again Koenig concentrated, the tip of his
finger touching detail, moving and then coming to rest
again. "Cut the first screen and spread two and three.
High magnification and diverse colour. I want an over-
lay for comparison."

"Any particular area?"

"H-7 on both."

"Coming up, Commander."

Bergman grunted as the screen changed, one transparency covering another, the details of each illuminated by lights that cancelled each other into darkness when blended. One point glowed an angry red.

"Something doesn't match, John. A boulder or heap of rubble is missing, but before or after the rescue?"

"It wasn't there before we made the search," said Koenig, manipulating the controls. "See? This was taken on the preliminary survey of the wreck. And this was taken when the dust had settled enough to give clear visibility. And now?" He thinned his lips as Sandra flashed another photograph on the screen. "It's gone. A boulder as large as an Eagle, and it simply vanished."

"It couldn't, John."

"If it was a boulder, I agree," said Koenig grimly. "My guess is that it was something else—a creature that had left the crater and gone into hiding. It stayed there while we bombed Schemiel. Then later it moved. Where would it head for, Victor?"

Bergman said, "Every living thing needs a source of energy in order to survive. Even that creature needs to eat."

"And where, aside from Alpha, can it hope to feed?" Koenig didn't wait for an answer. Rising, he strode to where Morrow sat at his console. "Paul, I want a complete scan of the area between Alpha and Schemiel. If anything is spotted moving, I want to know exactly where it is. Set up observation scanners and hook them up to a movement detector. Sandra, maintain a constant check on all vibratory and energy levels. Kano, have the computer determine all possible routes from Schemiel to Alpha, working on the basis of easy mobility."

"What kind of mobility, Commander?"

A good question—how did the thing move? "Assume that it crawls," snapped Koenig. "You've an idea as to its size, so some routes would be more suitable than others. Plot and search them. Once we know where it is, we can send Eagles against it."

To blast it with a hail of nuclear explosives. To hold

it fast with grapnels and hurl it into space. To get rid
of it one way or another. To destroy it—before it destroyed them.

Technician Ivan Beresova shone the bright circle
of his flashlight on the roof of the narrow cavern and
squinted at the sudden gleam of reflected light. A mineral deposit of some kind or a strata rich in silicone
—later it would be checked for potential value, but
for now it was enough to report the find.

"New?" The squad commander was notorious for
his attention to minute detail. "How new?"

Beresova sighed into his radio. "New, sir. It wasn't
visible the last time I looked. The blast could have
opened a crack as it caused debris to fall."

"Your position?" The leader grunted as Beresova
gave it. "You're pushing too far ahead. This isn't an
exploratory mission, but just a general surveillance
patrol. Return to point twelve and wait."

It was Beresova's turn to grunt. Roper was no cow-
ard, but at times he carried caution to an extreme.
Surely there could be no harm in finishing his examination of the area. As he remembered there was a
long gallery a little further on with scintillant crystals
imbedded in the roof. The blast could have jarred
some loose, and if he took some back with him Sonya
would be grateful.

He felt a warm glow as he thought of the girl—
tall, blonde, with a good figure and, more important
as far as he was concerned, she seemed to like him.
As a chemist she would be interested in anything he
found and, as a woman, she would more than appreciate the gift of unusual stones that could be turned
into jewellery.

"Ivan, do you hear me?" Roper was impatient. "Return to rendezvous and wait. I want no heroics, and
we're far enough from Alpha for anything but a major
fissuring to be unimportant."

"I hear you, sir."

"Then acknowledge. End examination and make for point twelve. Understand?"

"Message understood, sir. Am on my way to rendezvous."

The truth—Roper hadn't specified which direction he should take and the gallery wasn't far. A few minutes would make no difference and, if Roper turned awkward, he could always claim to have spotted an unusual deposit. And Sonya was worth the risk.

The cavern narrowed as he approached the far end, the walls closing to a mere crack, but still one large enough to pass him without any danger of snagging his suit. The floor was thick with debris, and once he stumbled as his foot turned on a shattered mass of loose stone. A turn and he squeezed around an adamantine column of basalt that by some geological freak stood among the softer material. Another hundred yards and he had entered the gallery.

In the gleam of his flashlight it shone with an eye-catching brilliance.

Minerals, twisted, distorted, confined beneath tremendous pressure and heat, fusing to adopt new and exotic structures to form gemstones of superb beauty.

The floor was littered with them, heaps jarred from their ancient resting place on the roof high above. It would take only a moment to stoop, collect a few and be on his way.

But there was too much choice.

Beresova moved from one heap to another, picking, selecting, seeing in his mind's eye the polished stones adorning Sonya's body. These for a necklace, and over there what could become a pendant, and a little deeper into the gallery for matching stones to grace shell-like ears. And it was important to take a variety, not just for their visual attraction, but because of their potential worth to Alpha. There could be diamonds or stones even harder than that particular form of crystallised carbon. Despite all their examinations and tests, the Moon remained to them a place of unexpected mysteries.

Then, as Beresova stooped to pick up a large stone, he felt it.

A vibration that came from the floor to travel up his fingers, to tingle his feet and send chills down his spine. A shaking that could portend a shifting of the Lunar crust, a fall, a new fissure suddenly gaping beneath his feet. A result of the blast, of course; it had to be. A fading seismological shock from the blast that had fused Schemiel, rendered frightening only because he was deep below the surface in a gallery that acted as a sounding board.

But suddenly he no longer wanted to be alone.

Beresova straightened up, turned, the circle of light thrown from his flashlight dancing over the walls and floor. He was standing close to a wall that suddenly split to send a shower of debris towards and around him. Shattered particles drifted around him, clouding his face-plate and turning the beam of his flashlight into a visible cone—a cone that danced and skittered over something that moved.

"External sector seventeen," said Morrow. "Level nine. That's way down deep, Commander."

A gallery buried far below the surface, away from the stars and the emptiness of space—a fitting place for a tomb.

Koenig looked at the schematic diagram, a muscle twitching high on one cheek. The designated point was a long way from Schemiel and far too close to Alpha for comfort. And the battle had opened with an advantage to the enemy. Ivan Beresova was dead, and somewhere in the base a woman grieved.

"Anything from Roper?"

"No, Commander. He heard a static blur, and when Beresova didn't respond he went looking for him. He found a tunnel in the gallery and the marks of something that had cleared the debris from the floor." He added after a moment, "There was no body."

That had gone, used as fuel to power the alien life of the creature that had come against them. One that could even now be pressing closer and closer to the heart of the installation—the atomic energy generators without which the entire Moonbase would perish.

Bergman said, "The creature is displaying intelligence, John. To go underground and to tunnel its way through rock towards the base must have been the result of a calculated decision."

"So?"

"And there is more proof in the way it left the crater. No ordinary animal would have taken advantage of the dust as it did. Can't you see that? To wait, to leave and to lie immobile until the area was clear. Then to find a fissure leading underground and in the direction of Alpha—John, that alien could have a higher intelligence than a man!"

"Is that why it kills? An intelligent entity would surely anticipate a hostile reaction."

"If it knew that it was killing, John." Bergman elaborated on the statement. "Each of the men who died was carrying some form of energy-using equipment —radios, lights, maintenance systems and the like. Their very brains transmitted a form of electronic impulses. For all we know, that alien was simply trying to gain the energy it needed to survive and simply didn't recognise the victims as independent entities. It absorbed energy as you might eat a grape. Would you know if the fruit was capable of feeling?"

And would he care if to refrain from eating was to die? A philosophical concept for which he had neither the time nor the inclination to pursue further. The base was threatened, to survive was the only thing that mattered, and Koenig was determined that Alpha should survive.

"Sandra?"

"Nothing, Commander." She turned from her instruments. "No vibration and no energy nodes. The entire area around Alpha is quiescent."

And would remain so until the thing decided to make its move.

"It seems to lie dormant each time it has ingested

food," said Bergman thoughtfully. "If we could find it at such a time, it could be relatively helpless. It might even be possible to communicate with it. John—"

"Forget it!" Koenig was harsh. "We can't afford the luxury of tolerance, not to that thing. Our job is to kill it, and fast. Paul?"

"Technical Section reports that all is as you ordered, Commander. Security is standing by with mobile weapons."

"Kano?"

"Computer checks out probable effects of the blast, Commander. There will be minor damage, but all tolerable. A mile further out and a hundred yards deeper and there would be none."

"That can't be managed." Koenig drew in his breath, knowing that he had done all he could, anticipated every known danger and guarded against it.

Known danger—but always there was the possibility that he had overlooked something, that a certain combination of elements would produce not an anticipated result, but something alien and frightening.

He said quietly, "Take over, Victor. If we fail, you'll have to use your own judgement. Paul, tell Helena I'm on my way."

She was waiting for him in Medical, looking very tense, her face betraying the conflict that he had engineered. A doctor's first duty was to the patient, but Koenig had demanded a higher loyalty.

"John, isn't there any other way?"

"None that I can think of—can you?" Then, as she remained silent, he said, "I've no choice, Helena. We're fighting the unknown and must use every weapon we have. Is she ready?"

"As ready as she'll ever be." She gestured to where Mathias stood beside Lynne's bed. "We've got her under twilight sedation. A blast of oxygen will snap her out of it. I'm not fond of the technique, but you insisted."

And he was the commander. Koenig caught the

note of accusation but ignored it. Later, if blame was to be apportioned, he would shoulder his responsibility and guilt.

The burden, perhaps, of a young girl's life.

Joining Mathias, he looked down at her. Her face was calm aside from the faint lines of tension that had appeared around the lips and eyes. The bone was more prominent than it should be, the skin a little too taut. A girl who, despite intravenous feeding, was displaying all the symptoms of one starving to death.

One he was going to use as bait.

The technicians had done well. Sprayed plastic had sealed the tunnel running from the Moonbase, and more sealed the cavern into which it led. A cavern too near for comfort, but the best they could do in the time available. Security guards, suited, armed with heavy weapons, stood beside the thick doors leading into the tunnel. More occupied various points against the walls. Beside them, carefully joined by snaking fuses, rested massed thermite together with conventional explosives and the dull bulk of a low-powered nuclear warhead.

Beside it stood a seismograph, crude but efficient, and delicate enough to register any near vibration. And there was food.

Dishes bore heaps of succulent viands, smoking meats, synthetic but enticing, vegetables, fabrications from the yeast vats and cholera tanks, fruits from the hydroponic farms, precious sugars.

"Commander!" A technician came to meet Koenig and his party as they entered the cavern. "Everything is in position as you ordered. The men have volunteered to remain."

"Thank them, but I must refuse the offer. Security will handle what needs to be done."

"But—"

"That is all. Withdraw your men and return to Alpha. Stand by on Red Alert."

Koenig watched them go. At his side Helena said,

"They mean well, John. We all want to see this work."

The gamble he had devised; the trap he had set and prayed would snap shut with a successful conclusion. Again he looked over the area, at the massed thermite, the explosives, the warhead itself. Food surrounded it.

"All right, Helena. Wake Lynne and then get back to Medical."

"My place is here, John."

"You're needed more there."

"Dr Mathias can take charge and you know it. Lynne Saffery is my patient. I blame myself for her condition, and no one is going to make me abandon her. I mean that, John."

Her sudden fury had transformed her from the normal, quietly efficient, emotionless machine dedicated to the art of healing into a woman resembling a tiger, one who would stop at nothing to gain her own way, one whose ancestors had ridden to war in open chariots ready to kill and die for the sake of their homes, their children, their men.

"As you wish, Helena. Brody?"

A security man turned from where he stood beside the seismograph. "Nothing as yet, Commander."

The thing, then, was still dormant, but it could not be too far away. The gallery where Beresova had met his death lay beyond and almost on a level with them, a matter of a few miles at most. And they were on a line from that point to where the great generators of Alpha turned out their oceans of power.

"Commander!" Brody was looking at the seismograph. "Something's happening!"

"Strong?"

"Yes. The needle's off the scale. It must be close."

"Abandon position! All to their stations! Helena, wake the girl!"

She writhed on the stretcher on which she had been carried, throwing her legs over the side, dropping to move with a sinuous, snake-like motion towards the plates of food. Koenig gripped her, felt her muscles contract beneath his hands as he held her firmly.

"Hungry," she whined. "I'm so hungry! Let me eat! I must eat!"

"Look at that food," said Koenig. "Look at it. A mountain of food just for the taking. Here, get a little closer, see it, smell it, touch it, taste it. Life, girl, life. Come and eat. Come and be fed."

Come and die if they had any luck at all. Respond to the bait and follow the urgings of the human brain that is registering your hungers. Telepathy was a reading of minds. A facility that Koenig hoped would work both ways. If Lynne could respond to the alien's hunger, then maybe it would respond to her pleasure at the sight of food.

And responding, it would be led through the fissures, rock, stone and crevasses into this cavern.

"Eat," he urged as he let the struggling girl inch towards the food. "Eat. See all the food there is waiting for you. All the wonderful energy. Just take it. It's waiting for you. Come and take it."

And come soon! Soon!

A bell rang from the seismograph and the floor shook a little. A shower of particles rained from the roof and a man, standing before a wall, said sharply, "It's coming! I can feel it!"

"Eat, girl, eat." Koenig waited as she snatched up a double handful of food and, as she thrust it into her mouth, swung her towards the tunnel. "Helena! Back to Alpha. Move!"

"Lynne—"

"Take her! Now get out of here! Everyone, get out!"

Trained, rehearsed, the guards knew what to do. Fire sparkled as fuses were lit and one man, running across the cavern, paused to jerk at something protruding from the atomic warhead. Another threw the contents of a flask over the device. It was a timing mechanism and some waste radioactives to enhance the central bait. Now all that remained was for the alien creature to follow the demands of its hunger drive.

As the massive doors closed to seal the cavern from the tunnel, Koenig felt his stomach knot with tension.

Success depended on a narrow margin of time. First some of the thermite to create an area of radiant heat, the rawest form of energy. Then the warhead, which he hoped would be swallowed, ingested, taken into the gaping maw he remembered. The conventional explosives that would bring down the walls and roof of the cavern, holding the thing fast and providing a barrier that would be fused solid by the rest of the thermite. And then the nuclear bomb itself, bursting with irresistible force, burning, searing, turning whatever the thing was made of into incandescent vapour, that vapour confined until the entire area would merge into a ball of plasmaclater to cool, to leave nothing but a spherical cavern coated with fused and glassy slag.

"John!" Helena turned as she ran, her face strained. "Lynne, I can't—"

Koenig caught the girl as she stumbled, throwing her over his shoulder in a fireman's lift, taking Helena's arm as they raced down the tunnel. Behind them came a dull boom as charges exploded to rip masses of rock to fill the opening. An added defence and a reenforcement to the doors.

More doors stood open ahead and they raced through and into a transport. As the capsule sealed and began to move, Koenig felt the first jar.

"The cavern," he said. "The walls and roof should be down by now."

"And the rest?"

The transport jerked in answer, a peculiar motion that seemed to take the vehicle and shake it before setting it down again. From all around came a deep rumbling as if a mighty organ was playing a bass note faraway. A note that grew louder, to tear the air, to snarl like the anger of a giant, to roar like the fury of a god.

"The nuclear bomb," whispered Helena. "John! Have we won?"

"I don't know." If the trap had worked the thing would be ash by now, gases that seethed in dying fury, its elemental atoms mixed with others, the whole rendered forever sterile.

But how to be sure?

"Commander?" Lynne Saffery blinked and strained against the pressure of his circling arm. He had automatically closed it around her when the shock had come; an instinctive gesture to protect the helpless. Now, looking up at him, she smiled. "This is nice, Commander, but how did we get here? Not that it matters, as long as we're together."

"Lynne!"

"Dr Russell!" She straightened, one hand lifting to touch her hair, blushing a little. "I'm sorry, Doctor. I didn't see you."

"How do you feel?"

"A little confused." The girl glanced from one to the other. "What happened? Did I walk in my sleep or something? Was the experiment a success?" She touched the soiled garment she wore. "Why am I dressed like this? Doctor, with all respect, I don't think I want to pursue any more investigations into my ESP attributes."

Koenig met Helena's eyes and felt himself relax. The encephalograph would confirm it, but he was convinced the girl's brain wave pattern was now normal —proof that the alien creature was dead, totally destroyed, the mental attachment formed between it and the girl now dissolved.

CHAPTER NINE

Edward Markham had long since decided that Constance Boswell was the most beautiful girl to be found on the Moon and now, watching her at work, he had no cause to alter his opinion. Moving over the soil, she had the appearance of a nymph, small feet seeming to float over the ground, her elfin face holding an enigmatic mystery. In the glow of the artificial sun, her hair shone with the gleam of polished gold.

Impulsively he said, "Connie, I love you. Why won't you marry me?"

"I will."

"When?"

"This day, that day, sometime, never." Laughing, she avoided his hands. "Be sensible, Edward. We both have work to do. Save romance for our recreation periods. Are you going to the dance tonight?"

"If you'll be there, yes."

"I'll be there."

"Then so will I." He watched as again she lowered the instrument she was carrying to the dirt, thrust the tip into the loam and triggered a switch on the handle. "What are you doing?"

"Checking for radioactivity, among other things. This is a very special piece of ground, or didn't you know?"

"Why else do you think I'm here." He moved a little, conscious of his purple sleeve. "We've had enough trouble with things coming from space without wanting more. That's why the commander ordered a security guard to stand watch."

"In case monsters spring from the ground like the warriors from Jason's teeth?"

"Jason's?"

"The teeth of the dragon that Cadmus slew and that Jason planted. Surely you know the story of the Argo?"

"I know it," he said, and took a step closer to where she stood. "But you've got it wrong. It's Cadmus's teeth, not Jason's."

"So, what's the difference? No matter what you call them, they still gave trouble." She tested another spot, triggered the results to register on the tape, then moved on. Below each point she tested rested a seed, their positions marked by a red tab. "How's Dennis?"

"He's fine."

"Tell him I asked after him when you see him."

"Tell him yourself. He'll be out and about tomorrow." Edward shook his head as he looked at the girl. "What does it take to make you aware I'm alive and waiting? A broken leg? Some bruises? A dose of radioactivity? All that happened to Dennis is that he didn't move fast enough and got himself hurt in the rock fall when that monster was cremated. If you want to feel sorry for anyone, then spare time for Sonya. She was really in love with Ivan."

"Yes, I know." Constance grew abruptly serious. "And I don't mean to tease you, Edward. It's just that, well, we're here and are going to stay here and it's stupid to get too involved. Why can't we just be happy together without wanting to own each other? Why do you have to be jealous all the time?"

"Because I love you, I guess."

"I know. And I like to hear you say it. Now move over and let me finish this."

Obediently he stepped out of her way and took up a position on the path. Above the sun glowed with a warmth he remembered when, as a boy, he had stolen time from school to go swimming in the local river, one still fit for such purposes if you ignored the broken glass and rusted iron that littered the bottom. Closing his eyes he could almost smell the rich scent of grass and trees, bushes and wildflowers and, with imagination, he could almost hear the hum of bees.

They would come, he thought, opening his eyes and looking at the neat plots, some covered with a fuzz of green now, others still waiting to support the crops soon to take root. On the far side of the cavern tiny figures worked on the wall, smoothing, gouging, turning blank stone into a work of art.

He might join them, he thought. Spend a few hours of his leisure periods giving a hand to the sculptors and artists. It would make a pleasant change from working in the maintenance section as a voluntary grease-monkey. Yet there was something about working on an Eagle that couldn't be beaten. To handle machinery so carefully designed, so functional in purpose, was to handle metal shaped as if it were a gem.

Idly he wondered if his request for a transfer from Security to Reconnaissance would be approved.

"Edward!" He heard the sharp intake of the girl's breath and spun towards her, his hand dropping to the laser holstered at his waist. "Edward! Look!"

He followed her pointing finger, stepping closer to gain a better view, seeing a dull, metallic-looking shape lying at the bottom of a hollow that she had cleared with her hands. A sphere as large as a grapefruit. One of the alien seeds.

"What is it? Danger of some kind?"

"No!" Her laughter was music. "I noticed a variation on the readings and decided to take a look. Can't you see, Edward? Don't you understand?" Her finger touched points on the surface of the sphere, tiny cracks that showed slight protrusions. "They're growing, darling! The seeds are growing!"

The music was from The Planets Suite—Saturn, The Bringer of Old Age. Leaning back in his chair, eyes closed, Koenig let himself sink into the magic of Gustav Holst's genius. He could almost taste the dust, smell the decay, feel the cobwebs of accumulated centuries, of aching millennia. Responding to the sonorous chords, his body felt the weight and burden of passing years, his mind became filled with the depression induced by remembered hopes and lost aspirations. As the music ended he sat with his mind drifting in a vast emptiness.

"John?" Helena Russell had come to sit beside him. Now, resting her hand on his own, she said, "John, what is worrying you?"

"Am I worried?"

"Of course. You are always worried about something, but I didn't mean that. This is something special. Your choice of music, for example. I'll admit the piece has an uplift at the end, but it's one that can easily be overlooked, the more so if the listener is in a state of acute anxiety. And I was watching your eyelids. When did you last have a psychological check-up?"

Smiling, he said, "Helena, don't you ever stop working?"

"Do you?" Returning the smile, she gently shook her head. "You're not a machine, John. You can be affected by strain and stress the same as the rest of us. What I'd like to prescribe for you is a nice long vacation."

"By the sea?" he suggested, entering into the spirit of the game. "Or high in the mountains so as to manage a little skiing? Or in the country somewhere? Where do you suggest, Doctor?"

"I'm serious, John. You know, the ancient Romans had more sense than they are usually given credit for. They knew the limitations of men. When they gave a general a triumph, they had a slave standing behind him to whisper in his ear, to remind him that, though he was being treated as a god, he was only a man and therefore mortal. Maybe you should have someone behind you all the time to remind you that you aren't a machine but only human."

"And liable to error."

"Of course—is there any human who isn't?" But she had grasped his meaning. "The seeds, John. You're worried about the alien seeds."

"Yes."

"Why? They seem harmless enough."

"They're growing." He turned to face her, the light catching the hard planes of his face, deepening the shadows in the concavities, turning his features into a mask of superficial hardness. "Helena, I'll be honest with you. I hoped the damned things wouldn't grow. I wanted them just to lie in the ground like stones and be equally harmless. I agreed to have them planted because I didn't want an argument with Victor. A weakness."

"No, John," she corrected, "a consideration for others."

"A gamble," he said bitterly, "and one I lost."

He was tired, she thought, as he leaned back in the chair. Tired, and more than tired; nerve and sinew held tense too long, mind given no respite from the endless necessity of having to make decisions, muscles responding with psychosomatic fatigue. And always would be the burden of responsibility, the isolation of command.

A holiday, she had suggested. A vacation in an impossible place where he could relax and forget and allow the hours and days to drift by without thought or concern. One day, perhaps they would be able to build such a place. Build one or find one, but even as she thought about it, she knew that for Koenig there could never be a true haven of rest. The most he could hope to obtain was a few snatched hours free of worry. The most she could do for him was to give him the strength of her trust.

And, at times like this, to try and lift his spirits, to edge him back from the depths of depression which, at times, yawned at his feet.

"What's new about the seeds, John? I know they're growing, but that's about all. Is there anything more than that?"

"Much more," he said grimly. "I'm waiting for a report from Nancy Coleman. Let's go and get it."

The botanist was in her laboratory and she wasn't alone. Victor Bergman turned and smiled as Koenig and Helena entered. He wore a thick apron and was busy with acids and vials.

"John! Helena! This will interest you! I've just verified Nancy's findings as to the chromosome count of the seeds. It's fantastic!"

As was everything else about the alien product— its rate of growth, the intricate root system, the oddly coloured sprouts and vestigial leaves. Koenig glanced through a window to where guards stood around the plot to keep watchers from the growths, which had now covered the dirt with a mass of convoluted spines and tendrils of brilliant hues.

Helena said, "What have you found, Victor?"

"Nancy discovered it during a routine check. We've been making tests at regular intervals, and finally she was able to isolate the basic structure. I—well, you tell them, Nancy."

"Thank you, Professor." The botanist put down a slide and turned to face the visitors. "As you know, chromosomes are to be found in every living organism, including bacteria. They contain the genes that determine the adult characteristics such as, in the case of a man, the hair colour, eye colour, height and so on, including any susceptibility to certain organic malfunctions and inherent defects, such as haemophilia. The numbers of chromosomes vary as to each species; the garden pea, for example, contains a total of eight—

four from each parent. A man contains forty-eight."
Pausing, she then ended by saying, "The plants out
there, from what I can determine, contain a dozen
times that number."

"What?" Helena frowned. "Are you certain?"

"No," admitted the botanist calmly. "That is why I
qualified my statement. There could be more, and I
suspect there are, but I am sure there are at least more
than five hundred."

Koenig said harshly, "Anything else?"

"Nothing really new, Commander." Nancy Coleman picked up a clipboard from the bench and ran
her finger down a list of notations. "The initial growth
was extremely high and is proof of the tremendous
concentration of energy held in each seed. The root
system is vascular, but it differs from the usual combination of xylem and phloem and is much more efficient. Chlorophyl is present, of course, but, again, there
seem to be additives that enhance the conversion rate
from received energy to carbohydrates. There is also
another compound manufactured, the nature of which
I have yet to determine. It is a complex molecular
chain that is concentrated in the centre and base of
the growth. There are also traces of cholesterol."

"Cholesterol?" Koenig frowned. "It's been a long
time since I studied botany, but I didn't think plants
contained cholesterol."

"They don't," said Nancy Coleman. "It's a sterol
found in animals. It's also a vitamin for insects." Her
finger moved down the list of notations. "I also found
a minute amount of choline."

Helena said thoughtfully, "That's a vitamin for
cockroaches. As I remember, it's also a constituent of
certain important fats, such as lecithin and acetyl-
choline."

"Yes."

"Do you usually find such a substance in plants?"

Before she could answer, Bergman said, "We are
dealing with something alien, Helena. We can't expect
it to be exactly like the plants we are familiar with.

It grew under a different sun and was subjected to different forces. We can only guess at its natural environment. All we know is that so far the growths display tremendous promise. The initial nutrient stored in the seeds, for example, and there could be fibres of incredible strength, medicines, fruits, saps of industrial value. All we can do now is wait."

"Wait for what, Victor?" Koenig turned from the window. His face was taut, the lines engraved as if with acid. "A plant," he said sombrely. "Yet one with a fantastic number of chromosomes. One with mammallian ingredients. One with a substance used by insects as a vitamin. What, in God's name, is growing out there?"

The spines straightened and swelled into leaves, each reaching upwards like a pleading hand towards the glowing disc of the artificial sun. The tendrils coiled into spirals of multi-coloured glory, looking like plaited ropes that moved to join, to merge, to change into a single complex flower. Beneath it rose a bole, swelling from the heart of the dissipated seed, a growth ringed with protective leaves edged with saw-like teeth. It resembled a marrow standing on end, the skin darkly green and traced with an elegant design in red and yellow. Quickly it grew to stand above the height of a man, the great flower at its summit held on a thick, flexible stalk, the open frond of petals turned towards the sun.

And then, unaccountably, the plants began to die.

Constance Boswell noticed it first, frowning over the readings of her electronic instrument, checking various points and then summoning Nancy Coleman.

The botanist shook her head when later she conferred with Victor Bergman.

"A general wilting, Professor. I can't as yet determine any particular cause. The water content of the soil is normal, and we have maintained the introduction of specific chemical fertilisers. Examination shows no obvious root damage."

"Could it be the natural end of their life-cycle?" Bergman shook his head. "No, of course not, even though alien the plants must serve some kind of purpose, if only that of perpetuating their own kind. Did you notice any formation of fruit or seeds of any kind either in the carpels or rind?"

"No."

"Then perhaps they need an energy-level change. Some plants need an environmental trigger to induce the final stage." He checked himself, aware of his limited knowledge, aware, too, that he was talking to an expert. "Or am I being stupid?"

"You could never be that, Professor," she said. "But each of us must stick to his own trade. I'd look like a perfect fool if I tried to argue with you about physics. But you are right, as it happens; chrysanthemums, for example, will only flower when the days and nights are of equal length. That's why they are so popular with nurserymen—they can bring them to bloom at any time they like simply by adjusting the lights. The alien plants could have something similar, but what stimulus shall we give them? Extra heat? Cold? Darkness? What?"

"Everything we can think of," said Bergman firmly. "I'll arrange to have the plot covered with an opaque seal and we can segregate the plants into sections. One we'll chill, another heat, a third we'll plunge into darkness, a fourth we'll flood and so on. Eventually we'll find the answer, Nancy. We've got to!"

But despite all they could do the plants continued to wilt. Only those that had been flooded showed a little strengthening, but it didn't last. Nancy Coleman, her eyes ringed with dark circles of fatigue, tested and checked and, in the end, admitted failure.

"There's nothing more I can do, Professor. If I could isolate a specific area of damage it would help, but there's nothing, just a general dehydration and loss of texture. The boles show no sign of developed progress, as you would expect if they contained seeds as does a melon, and the flowers are devoid of any sign of potential fruit. In any case, with only a single flower, I tend to think any seeds would be developed with the pod itself."

"You've tested the soil, of course?"

"Yes. A general debility of the untreated area, as is to be expected. The plants themselves don't bear luxuriant foliage. My guess is that they either originate in a loam of high fertility or are close to a forest of some kind. One with deciduous trees—the nourishment provided by the falling leaves would help to replenish the soil." Sighing, she added, "I'm guessing, of course. And it appears that I'm a bad guesser. It looks as if we've lost, Professor; unless a miracle happens, those plants are all going to die."

The miracle was named Constance Boswell.

Testing the soil was a routine task, one that had grown into a habit, her hands moving in unison with her feet, the instrument probing, her eyes less interested in the reading shown on the dials than in the plants among which she moved. Not negligence in the true sense, because the readings, recorded, would later be checked and correlated in the computer held in the botanical laboratory.

It was simply that she was young, undecided as to how deeply in love she was, and enamoured by the exotic growths.

One, in particular, she had made her friend.

It stood in a shadowed portion of the screened-off area, the great flower lowered now from where it had turned towards the sun, the leaves drooping, the tracery of the bole blurred a little, the colours not so bright as once they had been. A plant, and yet something about it appealed to her. The romance, perhaps, the thought of its long, long journey to this potential haven, to be planted, to grow, to fade just before it could reach its culmination.

The irony of life, she thought, standing before it. As her life had in a sense ended that black day when the Moon had been blasted from its ancient orbit and sent into new and frightening regions of space. How many had died since then who would normally have lived? How many lives had been changed, romances ended, loves lost? Who could tell of the plans that had been made, only to be discarded in the need for survival?

Did she really love Edward Markham?

Did he really love her?

Could anyone now afford to be in love at all?

Deep thoughts, but at least, there was comfort in a flower.

She smelled the perfume even as she thought of the bloom. It embraced her like a cloud, tantalizing odours filled with the nostalgia of long-lost days. The scent of violets and roses, of the clean crispness of sheets and the rich, dark scents of tar, the thin, slightly acrid smell of petrol, the ineffable fragrance of lilacs and carnations, of mint and sage and tobacco plants, of places she had known and events now barely remembered.

It was natural to lift her face and no surprise to see the bloom hanging from its stalk and suspended just above like a gathered curtain of lace filled with the soft effulgence of twilight and vagrant beams of golden illumination that touched and gilded and turned beauty into a heart-stopping loveliness for which she could find no words, only feeling.

And natural to stand while the great flower dropped lower to enfold her face and head in aroma and softness.

To stand and wait while memory spun and danced like the upstreaming sparks from a fire fanned by a sudden rush of wind so that all the universe became a thing of pleasure so intense that it verged on the unbearable.

And time became one long, drawn-out moment of exquisite ecstasy.

CHAPTER TEN

The flooding had failed, the chilling, the heating, the darkness and the light, the blasting with added energies, the irradiation, the sonic impulses directed from carefully designed projectors.

The plants were as good as dead.

Bergman looked at them, his face betraying his disappointment, one that grew as workers removed the screens and partitions. Koenig shared his sense of failure; despite his initial objections, the growing of the seeds had become a challenge, and in any conflict in which Alpha was involved, he was filled with the urge to win.

"Are they all like this, Victor?"

Bergman looked at the wilted leaves and shrunken boles and shrugged. "I'm afraid so. Connie runs the checks and she reported they were all the same. There is no point in maintaining the screens and wasting energy any longer. It was a chance and it failed."

"Did you retain any of the seeds?"

"No," admitted Bergman. "There seemed little point. Either they would grow or they wouldn't, and we are limited as to possible environments. And we had no way to tell how many were viable. As it was, less than fifty percent of the batch germinated." Again his shoulders lifted in a shrug. "Well, we can't be successful all the time. We simply have to accept failure now and again."

A fact that life had taught him and a philosophy that his mechanical heart aided him to accept. Koenig's heart was a thing of flesh, an engine of muscle, prone to all the emotions that have ever plagued mankind. For him there was and could be no excuse for failure. He could accept it, but he would never be able to like it.

Now, as the workers cleared the site, he looked at the bared plot and frowned. The plants reminded him of something, but for a moment he couldn't tell what. Then it came to him—an old painting he had once seen in a museum during one of his rare vacations. A scene of men standing, some lying, all stooped, weary, broken with struggle and fatigue.

"A battlefield," he said wonderingly. "Victor, it looks like a battlefield."

Almost totally cleared of the partitions, the plot was a mass of leaves, boles, flowers that had shed petals, roots that lifted above the ground to writhe like boneless fingers. Some, he noted, seemed to be strangling others, and the boles, taller than a man, held a humanoid appearance, the wilted flowers the crests of helmets, the fallen petals patches of blood, the elegant traceries the markings of gaudy uniforms. The accoutrements of men who had once marched defiantly into battle, more concerned with how they looked than the possibility of mutilation and death.

He could almost hear bugles.

"Victor?"

"A battlefield," admitted Bergman. "You are right, John, but that is exactly what it is. Those plants must have fought for the maximum of food and water, of room in which to expand, of sunlight to call their own. The law of the jungle—kill or be killed, live or die. A survival trait that even a plentiful supply of water and fertilisers couldn't eradicate. And we must have missed something, some essential element or ingredient they needed in order to survive." His hands clenched in frustrated anger. "If only we had known what it was!"

His anger was a betrayal of the emotion that even a mechanical heart couldn't wholly eradicate; the anguish of the dedicated scientist who has new knowledge within his grasp, only to lose it because of a little ignorance.

Koenig said, "Has Nancy thought of taking cuttings, Victor?"

"She's thought of everything, John, but it simply isn't possible to do as you suggest. Every plant examined so far shows the same deterioration. They are dying, are dead despite their appearance. The internal tissue is contracting, the sap has ceased to run, the roots are nothing more than extensions of inert tissue. I—" He broke off as the last partition was removed. "John!"

Koenig had seen it.

A plant standing tall and firm among the others, the flower a disc of lambent colour, the bole swollen and graced with red and yellow.

One plant, the victor, and again he almost heard bugles.

"But how?" Bergman shook his head. "The girl reported they were all the same. She must have lied or been mistaken. But how could she have missed seeing that plant, John? You realise what this means?"

His hopes restored, a second chance of success, the door to fresh knowledge again set ajar. But Koenig didn't look at him, nor at the exotic growth, but at the girl who came from behind the plant.

"Connie!"

She took a step forward as he called. Against the rich darkness of the distended bole she looked very slight and very pale.

For a moment she wavered and then, taking another step forward, said in a small voice, "You mustn't hurt it. You won't hurt it, will you? Promise not to hurt it."

"The plant?"

"You mustn't touch it. I've had to keep it hidden. I won't let you hurt it." The thin, small voice rose to a scream. "I won't let you hurt it! I . . . please! Please! Please! Please. . . !"

Koenig caught her as she fell.

Helena closed the file lying on the desk before her, leaned back in her chair, palmed her eyes and, as she lowered her hands, said, "I don't begin to understand this, John, but Constance Boswell is apparently suffering from the terminal stages of pernicious anemia."

"Anemia?"

"It seems incredible, doesn't it?"

"Could there be a mistake?" Koenig was baffled. "When did she have her last physical?"

"Ten days ago. She worked with radioactive isotopes and I checked her for any contamination. Results negative. Since then she has been working full-time with the Botanical Section under Nancy Coleman. I've checked and she hasn't been anywhere near a source of radioactivity. In any case, the anemia wouldn't have progressed so fast and so far and, had it been due to contamination, there would have been other symptoms. As I said, John, I don't begin to understand it."

"Can you cure her?"

A question Edward Markham repeated as, together with Dr Mathias, she and Koenig joined him where he waited patiently beside the patient's bed. He was, Koenig noticed, sitting very close, the thin fingers of the girl held fast in his own.

"We can save her," promised Helena. "It will take massive transfusions of fresh blood and she will need care and rest, but she'll be all right, given time. The main thing is to prevent a recurrence of the condition. You know her well, I understand."

"I'm in love with her."

"Which makes her a very fortunate young woman. You, then, naturally see her often. When was the last time?" Helena frowned at the answer. "So long? Did your duties keep you apart?"

"No, it's just that for days now she hasn't wanted to see me. She claimed that she was busy all the time with those damned plants—I'm sorry Commander, Doctor."

"Forget it," said Koenig. "So she said she was too busy to see you. Was she? I mean, did you check in any way?" Then, as the young man hesitated, he said, "I'm not accusing you of violating her privacy, but only of acting like a man in love. Did she spend much time with the plants?"

"All of it." Markham looked at where the girl lay. "She wasn't lying in the sense that she was busy, but only in the sense that she didn't have to be. She didn't have to actually work if she hadn't wanted to be with me. She didn't have to lie. I wouldn't have liked it and I would have argued a little, but, hell, I love her and what she wants is all I care about. Dr Russell, is there anything I can do?"

"There isn't at the moment. You haven't the same type blood, so I can't use you as a donor, but we have all we need. Just leave her with us now. When she's better she'll want to see you, I'm sure. Bob?"

Mathias said, "Come on, lad. Let's get on with the job. And how about you? Haven't you anything to take care of?"

Work was the best antidote for grief. Koenig said, "Report to maintenance, Edward. They could use a hand in stripping an Eagle, and you're good at the job. And Carter's running a simulator course. Ask him nicely and maybe he'll let you sit in on it."

He stepped back as the young man left the ward and orderlies came forward wheeling equipment. As Mathias set to work, he gestured Helena to her office.

"Anemia," he said when they were inside. "It's almost like saying the girl has a fit of the vapours.

How long has it been since you treated a case of anemia?"

"A long time, John."

"Which means it's rare?"

"No. It means that now it's very easy to treat. We cure it by means of injections of liver extract and vitamin B-12. I'm talking of normal anemia, you understand, not that caused by cancer, such as leukaemia."

"And there's no doubt the girl isn't suffering from that?"

"None." Her voice hardened a little. "I appreciate your concern, John, but I do know my job."

"Did I say you didn't?" He flared with a sudden anger, but he quickly suppressed it. "I'm sorry, Helena, but I need to be certain. The thing's a mystery. She didn't do anything or go anywhere aside from tending those plants. And you didn't see her as I did—dazed, crazed, too weak to stand. Something caused her to act like that, and I have to find out what it was. How long will it be before she can be questioned?"

"Not long, John. I'll let you know."

The battlefield was deserted, the workers gone, the entire area empty aside from watchful security guards. On the plot of ground the alien plants looked withered, shrunken, many missing where the botanists had reaped their harvest, boles and flowers and tissue taken to be sectioned and sealed and stored for later examination. Specimens snatched from dissolution, a poor reward against what might have been.

Koenig could not help but be impressed.

The single survivor had been shrouded in a room of its own, plastic sheeting hiding it from casual view, the upper transparency allowing the passage of actinic light that Nancy Coleman was certain was essential to its continued development.

"Now that it is nearing maturity, it will need all the energy it can get. Water, too, of course, and nutrients, but nothing can replace actual light. It is obvious now that it uses photosynthesis just as our own plants do. Now, if only it were possible to isolate the incredible growth-factor, then we would have solved the problem of a food supply for all time."

She glanced at the plant, lost in a dream, her eyes filled with the reflected thoughts of wheat as high as trees, of potatoes as large as pumpkins and grown in a matter of days.

Bergman was engrossed in something else.

"I've been monitoring the internal sounds, John," he said as Koenig joined him where he stood beside the great bole. "Whatever's happening in there is very active. Listen." Attaching a suction microphone to the wall of the bole, he threw a switch, and from the speaker of the amplifier he held, Koenig heard a series of oddly disturbing noises. They resembled liquid gushings, slithers, murmurs, the beat of something that could have been a heart.

"Pumps?"

"Possibly," said Bergman. "Plants normally circulate their fluids by osmosis, but this obviously has developed a different system. It could account for the phenomenal continuance of growth after the initial stages."

"Didn't you spot any pumping mechanism before?" Koenig listened again to the sound. "Something like a heart?"

"No, John, we didn't. And the sound you are now hearing is comparatively recent. It could be that the pumping system previously used was of a different order, perhaps a series of small impulses that would merge into a common blur. And that's another thing. The plant seems to be growing in a series of metabolic jumps. It's almost as if it changes its nature as it goes along—like a beetroot, which turns into a potato, a pea, an ear of wheat, a melon. I'm exaggerating, but the analogy holds. It's almost as if it's adapting to fit its environment."

"Adapting?" Koenig was thoughtful. "As a cactus,

say, would adapt to a moist climate in order to survive?"

"Exactly."

"And is this common?"

"I don't know, John." Bergman spread his hands in a helpless gesture. "I'm not a botanist. Some of the lichens, perhaps, but I'm only guessing."

Nancy Coleman corrected his guess.

"No plant—and that includes the lichens and even the algae—can change like that, Commander. They are governed as we are by their genetic structure. You wouldn't expect a man to grow wings in order to adapt to a mountainside life, would you? Or claws? Or develop webbed feet because he lives in a marsh? No, of course not, and a plant is as rigid in its development. Some things they can do—they can lie dormant for long periods of time waiting for a favourable environment. They can apparently die and spring to life from encysted spores—and now I am talking about the simplest plants, you understand. But they can't change from one species to another."

"As this alien does?"

"As it appears to do," she corrected. "We don't have any information as to its natural growth progression, so all we can do is make intelligent guesses. And," she added pointedly, "some of them aren't so intelligent."

"Like the thing developing a heart?"

"Plants don't have hearts," she snapped. "Don't let your imagination run away with you, Commander. Plants don't have hearts, no matter what you may hear from inside."

No hearts and no insect vitamins, either, but this thing contained elements only to be found in animal and other forms of life. He thought of the lepidoptera, the order that contained butterflies and moths, the larvae of which fed on plants. Did this thing contain another parasite? Would Alpha again be menaced by an alien creature almost impossible to destroy?

"John!" Bergman had seen his face and the expression it carried. "Is something wrong?"

"I don't know, Victor, but there could be." Koenig lifted the commlock from his belt. "Security, send extra men to Rural Area One. Personal armour and heavy equipment. Have semi-portable lasers set up at the entrance to the cavern and at strategic points inside." He added after a moment, "And set mines in the entrance ready to explode on order. I want charges heavy enough to bring down the roof."

"You're afraid of something," said Bergman as Koenig lowered the commlock. "But, John, it's only a plant. It can't hold anything really dangerous. For one thing, it isn't big enough."

"How large is a virus, Victor?"

"It's very small, John." Bergman got the point. "But it can kill despite its size. You're right, of course; we mustn't take chances. But look at it." He gestured towards the plant. "It has a unique beauty. How can such a thing hold terror?"

A question only time could answer, but, guided by the gesture, Koenig's eyes studied the alien growth with a sharpened suspicion. The leaves, once edged with saw-like teeth, now hung like a drape of silken veils at the foot of the bole. The great flower drooped on the end of its stalk, the petals frayed like tassels, the colours those of old tapestries. The bole, darkly green, seemed to have enhanced the contrast of the elegant traceries, the patterns of red and yellow more prominent now, deeper, wider.

Like the cracks starring the shell of an egg and growing even as he watched.

"John!" Bergman stared his disbelief. "It's opening! The bole is opening!"

Splitting along a thousand lines of fracture, the pieces supported now only by a delicate inner membrane, the entire side of the bole facing them now starred and flaking.

"Nancy?"

"It could have reached fruition, Commander. Don't

get too close. Many plants have some form of ejection mechanism for their seeds. This could be one of them."

Accumulated gases used to literally fire the seeds far from the parent growth. Organic springs that would fling them like stones from a sling. Vapours, even, designed to stun or kill any hungry predator—who could tell what defence mechanisms had been developed in an alien world?

They should run, but nothing would have dragged the botanist from where she stood busy with her camera. Nothing would have pulled Bergman from the chance to observe what had never been seen by man before. And he, like the others, was expendable should the worst happen and the security guards be forced to destroy the cavern and all it contained.

"Look!" breathed Bergman, entranced. "Look!"

A flake fell from the bole, another, a rain of thick, green particles that rustled as they fell to form a mound on the drape of leaves. An opening showed, widening even as they watched, an oval space over six feet in height and four feet in width. A gaping orifice that revealed an inner compartment lined with strands softer than any silk forming a roseate nest that cradled the incredible.

"A woman!" Shocked, Nancy Coleman lowered her camera. "A woman—but in God's name, how?"

Koenig said nothing, watching, looking at the shape held snugly in the cradle of roseate moss. A girl—the loveliest he had ever seen.

CHAPTER ELEVEN

They named her Enalus—the child, if not of the sea, then of space, that great ocean of emptiness between the stars—and she was beautiful.

Beautiful beyond all visions of loveliness, a fact confirmed by his eyes and one to be added to another verified by his brain. She was beautiful and she was more alien than anything he had previously known.

A thing Koenig found hard to accept as he watched her in Medical Centre, moving to Helena's direction, her small, high-arched feet carrying her with a dancer's grace.

"Again? Of course, Dr Russell, anything you wish."

Her voice was softly resonant, echoing in the mind like the distant sound of chiming bells, plucking at the strings of emotion so that he responded to her attraction as if to a thing of delicate wonder beyond the concept of price.

"And again?" She moved like a wisp of perfumed cloud. "And again?"

Exercises to check her coordination, the cold eyes of scanning instruments following her every gesture as others sniffed the air and her body with electronic

nostrils. She ignored them, turning, the mane of glow-
ingly roseate hair streaming like a dawn-touched
waterfall from the high curve of her brow, rippling
over the soft roundness of her shoulders. Beneath the
simple garment she wore, the lines of her figure were
prominently feminine; the mound of her breasts
sharply delineated by the narrow construction of her
waist, the swell of hips and thighs, the taper of
calves and ankles.

Her face was angelic—soft lips, gentle eyes, ears
like shells, a chin touched with a dimple, nostrils made
to be touched, a brow designed to be stroked, skin that
yearned for kisses as her hands with the delicate fingers had been made for caresses and . . .

"John!" Helena's voice cut through his reverie and
Koenig started, conscious that he had been day-
dreaming, lost in a world of imagination. "I've finished
for the time being. You can have Enalus taken back
to her room now."

"Must I be locked away, Commander?" She took a
step towards him, hands lifted in mute appeal. "I get
so lonely at times and it has been so long. Why must
I be shut away in a prison?"

"For protection," said Helena. "Yours and ours."

"Commander?" She ignored the comment. "That's
so cold, isn't it? May I call you John? Helena calls you
that; may I?" She smiled at his nod, her face irradi-
ated as if from within by a glowing luminescence.
"That's wonderful! You are so kind to me, John. You
are all so kind. But why must I be kept shut away as
if I were a prisoner? What harm have I done you?
What harm could I do? Please, John, couldn't I be
allowed a little freedom?"

It was incredible to think that she had come from
a plant. Even more incredible that she should have
the power to communicate as she did with words of
such familiarity. An ability she had demonstrated from
the very first when she had stepped from the opened
bole to stretch and smile and extend her hands to
those watching as if she had been a traveller at the

end of a long voyage who had just arrived to be greeted by friends.

"John?"

The siren call of her voice laved him with its warmth and intimacy, hinting of secrets shared and episodes to come, of promises unspoken but implied.

With an effort he said, "No, Enalus, not yet."

"But, why, John? Why?"

"Because you are strange to us, as you must know. We have to be careful. Alpha must not be put at risk. I . . . well, just be patient for a little while longer. I promise you it won't be long. You can trust me for that, Enalus. Just be patient for a little while longer."

He was babbling and knew it, but a part of him was unable to halt the spate of words. Beyond the girl he could see Helena, the disapproval on her face. An emotion not matched by Mathias, who stared as a man entranced.

"John, will you summon security, or shall I?" Helena lifted her commlock.

"No." Koenig turned and clenched his hands and felt the nails drive into his palm. The pain cleared his head a little, giving him a measure of detachment so that, when he turned again to face the little group, he was able to speak with direct firmness.

"Helena, take Enalus to her room. Make certain she is secured."

"John! Please! You promised—"

"After you have done that, summon Victor to join us here."

"John?"

Without looking at her, Koenig said, "I haven't forgotten my promise, Enalus. You'll be given more freedom as soon as I'm certain you present no danger to the Moonbase. Until then I'm taking no chances. Now please be sensible and cooperate. Do you need help, Helena?"

"No."

"An orderly, perhaps?"

"I can manage."

Koenig sagged a little as she ushered the girl from the chamber. Watching him, Dr Mathias said softly, "Did she get to you, Commander?"

It would have been stupid to lie.

"Yes. And you?"

"Me, too." Mathias drew in his breath and released it with an audible sigh. Then he said quietly, "What the hell have we got here?"

"Something alien."

"I know, but when you're with her you tend to forget that. She seems more human than any other human I know. And she's lovely with it—that hair, those eyes, that figure, that skin! Men dream about such things and try to put their thoughts into words. They call it poetry. Others make songs and paint images and still more can do nothing but sit and think and think and destroy themselves with hopeless longing. I've seen them. Pathetic creatures who are obsessed. We call them mad." Again Mathias drew in his breath. "Is that what we have here—a source of madness? Or have we found an angel? Which, Commander? Which?"

Bergman listened to the silent humming of the tape and looked at the others. "Well, that's one problem solved. Enalus isn't using vocal communications at all. If she had, her voice would have registered on the recorder."

"Telepathy?" Koenig switched off the machine. "So she's reading our minds."

"Not necessarily. All she needs to do is to bypass the normal vibratory sequence of sound communication and impinge her words directly on the receptors of the cortex. She would reverse the procedure in order to understand what you were saying. Imagine using radios instead of ears and tongues. In fact, the use of suit-radios is a good analogy." Frowning, he added, "But it still doesn't explain how she knew the language. She could have learned it from someone, perhaps, but whom?"

"I can answer that, Victor." Helena glanced at Mathias. "From Constance Boswell. Right, Bob?"

"We can't be certain of that, Doctor."

"But the evidence points to it." From among the papers littering the desk she produced a file. "This is Connie's. I won't read it, but the facts are plain. After the initial examination and emergency transfusions, another examination was made during which a pattern of tiny punctures was found on the scalp previously hidden by the hair. The penetration was to the bone. There was no blood. On the sides of the face we found a peculiar abrasion. I thought it to be beard-rash; then I remembered that Edward Markham was closely shaven."

"And he hadn't been close to her for days before she collapsed." Koenig narrowed his eyes in thought. "A connection?"

"We know that she lied about the condition of the plant," said Bergman. "That could have been an instilled protective device. If so, there must have been some form of contact. My guess is that the flower could have caused the punctures and, if it did, there could have been some form of mental contact."

"Between a girl and a plant?" Koenig waved a hand to dismiss the anticipated explanation. "All right, I know. The thing is alien, so normal experience doesn't apply. So somehow it read her mind and gained a knowledge of the language at least. And what else?"

Bergman said slowly, "An image."

"Victor?"

"A pattern, then, if you like. Something on which to build whatever was being formed in the pod. Haven't you noticed the similarity?" He glanced from Koenig to Mathias and raised his eyebrows. "No? I spotted it from the first and so did Nancy. There is a striking resemblance between Enalus and Constance Boswell. They could almost be sisters—but one is far more refined and enhanced than the other. More attractive in every way. Yet the basic similarities are there. You agree, Helena."

"Superficially they are, but it is only skin-deep. As yet I've found it impossible to take X rays of Enalus —her body is opaque to any form of scanning. She apparently has no blood; the tissue beneath the skin is a homogeneous mass of fibroid and the skin itself is more of a flexible layer than a true epidermis. The navel is a mere indentation, as to be expected, and both secondary and primary sexual features are non-functional—that is, she could neither give birth to a child or suckle it if she did."

"She must eat," said Bergman. "Does she?"

"Yes—that function, at least, seems normal. Her ingestion of solid and liquid matter is that of a young, healthy girl with a good appetite." Helena added dully, "She also has a perfect set of teeth—or would have if it were not for a minor irregularity in the upper left molar. Constance Boswell has exactly the same irregularity."

More proof, if it were needed, that the girl had been used as a pattern by whatever forces had determined the shape of what grew within the bole of the alien growth. And if there had been no pattern?

Pollination, thought Koenig. Plants, like animals, were bisexual. A flower needed to be fertilised before a plant could bear fruit and, even though the growth had been alien, the same principles could apply. Had the other plants died because they had not been stimulated into entering the final stage of their life-cycle?

Bergman cleared his throat and said, "Well, so far, so good. We know, or can make a reasonable assumption, how Enalus gained her knowledge of the language and how she communicates. We can also have a fair idea of how she comes to look as she does. The question now is—what do we do with her?"

She had been placed in a room at the end of a residential corridor, the other chambers empty now, the passage secured by a pair of guards. They snapped to attention as Koenig approached and he acknowledged their salute before passing on to halt at the sealed door. For a moment he stood before it, then lifting his commlock, he fired the stream of electronic particles that triggered the catch.

Closing the panel behind him, he turned to look at Enalus.

She lay on the bed, her legs sprawled in an elegant disregard for normal convention, the long, smooth lines of her thighs gleaming like pearl in the glow of the lights. She had slit the sides of the gown she had been given and adjusted the neck so that it hung in appealing folds, catching the eye and leading it to the double swell of her breasts.

Or, he reminded himself, savagely, the mounds of tissue that gave the appearance of breasts. But it was hard, so hard, to think of her as other than human.

"John?" She turned to face him, her elfin face wreathed in the mane of her hair, the eyes like lambent pools beneath the arc of her brows. "Do you want me, John? You did say I could call you that."

"Yes, Enalus, I did."

"And?"

"We've been talking about you. Or perhaps you know that."

"How could I know, John?" Did the sweet resonance of her voice hold a tinkle of mockery? "How could I know what you have been doing?"

"Don't you read minds?"

"No." She straightened with a swirl of material, hair flying, strands deftly swept back by a lifted hand. "Why should you think that? I speak and you hear my words. You speak and I hear mine. But what you think and how you feel—those things are a mystery to me." Her face brightened a little. "My freedom, John? Did you come to give me that?"

"What would you do with it, Enalus?"

"Enalus. That is a nice name. I haven't yet thanked you for giving it to me. My freedom?" She paused and sat with her hands locked around one uplifted knee,

Aureoled by the light, her hair glowed like a crest, a halo around the small neatness of her skull, the delicate structure of her face. "I wish to learn," she said, after a moment. "There is so much to learn. And I need to grow."

"To grow?"

"In wisdom," she said quickly. "Is that how I should say it? To grow in wisdom. To gain understanding. To increase my stature. Words! They are so limited. How I wish that you could understand me with a thought or that I could you. Words are so very slow, so slow. John, why did you send me here with Helena?"

He blinked at the sudden question, not expecting it, surprised that she should have considered the matter important enough to have remembered.

"I thought it best, Enalus."

"And what you think best, you do. This much already I have learned about you, John, as I have learned that all are different in small ways. Helena is different from you and Bob is darker and Victor is older and Nancy is as old but different again. Why is that, John?"

"We have two sexes and are of different ages. Also, there are various races among us."

"But you are basically all the same," she said, wistfully. "You are all human."

Which is something you are not and can never be, he thought, and felt a sharp regret at the coldness of the truth. A regret rendered the more poignant by the realisation that, of them all, she would be the most alone—a solitary member of her species who could never find her way home, a lost waif whose world might be nothing more now than a cloud of cosmic dust. It would be such a small thing to give what comfort they could. To help her. To pretend that she had a right to belong.

"John?" Enalus slipped from the bed and stood before him, looking very demure, very fragile and helpless, very young and alone. "Is the door to be opened? Am I to be allowed to mix with the others? Please!"

"Yes," he said. "You are. That's what I came to tell you."

The decision insisted on by Bergman, who had hammered home the need to learn, to observe, to reap what knowledge could be gained while they had the chance. Mathias had backed him; Helena had not. She was waiting in the passage, coming to join him after he had given instructions to the guards.

"You told her, John?"

"Yes."

"You should have given her a key," she said bitterly. "The key to Alpha. What would it be, John? A laser? The master component of Main Control? Or should we all have put our necks on a block?"

"Precautions will be taken," he said patiently. "She will be accompanied at all times and only allowed access to certain parts of the Moonbase. Damn it, Helena!" he flared as he saw her expression. "What else should we do? Lock her in a cage?"

"That or plant it in a garden." She halted and met his eyes. "*It,* John. No matter how that thing looks, it isn't human. It came from a plant and it robbed the brain of a girl. And it—"

"You don't like her," he interrupted. "You hate her."

"No, John," she said after a moment, "I don't hate her. You can't hate something so alien—not if you are rational. But you don't have to trust it, either. Enalus will cause trouble; I'm sure of it."

He smiled, trying to lighten the situation. "Woman's intuition, Helena?"

If so, it was accurate. Three days later Edward Markham was dead.

CHAPTER TWELVE

He was found in his room, lying supine on the unused bed, one hand lifted to rest above his head, his cheeks drawn and paper-pale.

"Anemia." Helena gave the diagnosis later after she'd examined the body in Medical. "At least that is the clinical definition of his condition. No sign of injury, no toxins, no signs of organic breakdown. Just a classic case of acute anemia. John, this is incredible!"

"Why?"

"A person doesn't get anemia overnight. Edward was fit and healthy; otherwise, he would never have been accepted as a security officer. He was in top condition when last seen a few hours ago, and yet, when called, he was dead. Dead, John! Dead from something that couldn't poss'bly have killed him so soon. Anemia doesn't work like that."

"Not even if accelerated?"

"No! Unless—" Helena broke off, frowning, then said slowly, "Anemia is a shortage of red corpuscles, and so a shortage of haemoglob'n in the blood. Which means, in turn, that the body is unable to extract oxygen from the air sucked into the lungs and transport it around the body."

"And a shortage of oxygen would lead to literal asphyxiation in the sense of being denied viable air. Could some form of vapour have done it, something like carbon monoxide, for example?"

"It could, but it didn't. Any gas or irritant vapour would have left traces. I found none."

"And if the anemia had been accelerated?"

"In that case I guess the result would have been what we see—sudden death, accentuated pallor and a complete absence of haemoglobin." Helena turned and took three steps across the floor, then turned again, her eyes haunted. "But, John, what you're talking about is impossible. You can't accelerate the progress of a disease or organic malfunction to such a degree. It means compressing weeks, months even, into a few hours. In that case there would be signs of malnutrition, but there aren't any. Edward Markham was fit when he went into his room and dead a few hours later. Something must have killed him."

Constance Boswell had no doubt as to what it was.

"It's that thing," she said. "Enalus. He couldn't take his eyes off her. Ever since he was given guard and observation duty, he's talked of nothing else. How lovely she is, how graceful, how gentle, how understanding. The bitch!"

"Steady!" Helena checked her pulse and looked over the bed at Koenig. "How did you know he was dead?"

"Edward? I heard some of the orderlies talking and I got up and saw him as they wheeled him from the examination room." Tears shone in the girl's eyes, glistening like pearls as they ran down her cheeks. Still weak from her own ordeal despite the strength given by the massive transfusions, she had little control over her grief. "Why?" she demanded. "Why did it have to happen to him? We had plans and . . . and . . ."

Helena gripped her hand as the girl shook with a storm of weeping.

As it subsided, Koenig said, "Connie, when Edward came to see you, did he say anything about Enalus?"

"Only how wonderful she was and how everyone envied him being one of her escorts."

"Nothing else? I mean, you two were in love and—"

"Were in love," she snapped bitterly. "How right you are, Commander. The past tense applied as soon as he saw that creature. He tried to pretend, but I could tell. He was enamoured of her and couldn't think of anything else. Even when he kissed me he was thinking of her—I could tell it." Her eyes filled again with tears. "Edward," she murmured brokenly, "I was a fool, but I wasn't sure. He loved me and I wanted him to love me, but there was no hurry and now it's too late. He's dead and that thing killed him. She killed him, Commander—and it's up to you to do something about it!"

A demand he couldn't refuse and a duty he had already acted on. And yet the mystery remained. Edward Markham had been on escort duty. Together he and Enalus had listened to music in the music room, had played a game of table tennis in the recreation room and later watched several pairs of wrestlers competing in the inter-section judo competitions. He had handed over his charge, reported to Security, had been relieved and had gone directly to his room.

"That would have been about eleven, Commander," said the guard who had taken over from Markham. "Maybe a little later. As you know I was on duty at the time and only caught a glimpse of him as he left my vicinity."

"And Enalus was with you?"

"Yes." George Tomlinson was broad, hard, his eyes deep-set and very direct. "She wasn't out of my sight until she went to her room."

"And you stood on guard?"

"Until relieved, yes. That was before she awoke. I went off duty after catching a snack and playing a little poker with some of the boys. You can check if you like."

"I have." Koenig was grim. "So you are willing to swear that Enalus was nowhere near Markham at the time he died?"

"I am."

From where she stood behind Koenig at the desk, Helena said, "What do you think of her?"

"Enalus?" Tomlinson shrugged. "She's just a girl."

"You're not in love with her?"

"I—no, of course not, Doctor. To me she's just a job of work."

Koenig nodded dismissal, and after the man had left the office he said, "Why did you ask him that, Helena?"

"I wanted to know something."

"And?"

"I found out what I wanted to know. He lied, John. That man lied!"

Her voice held a throbbing intensity, emotion far in excess of what the discovery called for and totally at variance with her normal calmness. A blend of anger and, he thought, more than a little fear.

Quietly Koenig said, "So he lied a little, Helena. You embarrassed him, perhaps, but what does it matter?"

"Don't you understand?" Her eyes met his own, direct, accusing. "He's in love with that thing, and so is every man on the Moonbase who's come in contact with her. But, worst of all, John, you are in love with her yourself!"

Nancy Coleman finished her coffee, looked thoughtfully into the empty container, then tossing it aside, said, "The word is metamorphosis, Professor, as you well know, so please don't try to flatter an old woman."

"Old, Nancy?" Bergman smiled and shook his head. "I can give you—well, too many years. And you know how age erodes the memory. Metamorphosis, of course—the period of rapid transformation from one form to another. But in plants?"

"In insects, not plants. It's the change made by a larval to an adult form such as a caterpillar to a butterfly. The caterpillar eats until it's ready, spins a cocoon, seals itself inside and waits. Then something happens and it changes into a butterfly, which breaks out of the cocoon and usually eats it before flying away."

"As a source of food," murmured Bergman. "As the alien creature did the pod in which it arrived."

She said shrewdly, "You're thinking of Enalus. Professor, there's no connection. She is the fruit of a plant, simply that and nothing more. An unusual-looking fruit, I'll agree, and one with fantastic attributes, but a fruit all the same. One shaped by the initial stimulus that fertilised the plant, as the commander suspected. A pity we didn't know that earlier; we could have fertilised them all."

With results Bergman would rather not think about. One other, yes, science demanded at least that, but more would have been tempting a destructive fate. And there could be no need. Each single fruit could perhaps be sufficient to itself.

Nancy shrugged when he asked the question. They sat in her laboratory and the light from the overhead sun caught her hair and turned the silver strands into gold.

"It's possible that she could bear other fruit, Professor, but how would you go about planting her? I hardly think you'd be allowed to bury her in the ground." She added after a moment, "Not by the men, at least; the women would probably dig the hole for you and fill it in with their bare hands."

"They dislike her that much?"

"Dislike is a mild word, Professor. Say they *hate* her and you'd be closer to the truth. Can't you guess why? She's competition. Five engagements have been broken since she's had the run of Alpha. Married couples are talking of divorce. No girl stands a chance when

Enalus is around, and she makes every woman feel and look second-rate. And there is Edward Markham's death."

"She can't be blamed for that."

"No?" Nancy Coleman shrugged. "Maybe not, but the women are certain she was the cause."

An illogical reaction and one that Bergman didn't want to discuss.

He said, "When Enalus stepped from the bole, you took photographs of her. I've taken some since and I'd like to make a comparison if I could use your equipment."

"Help yourself." The botanist waved to the far end of the laboratory. "The left-hand panel is static; the right-hand one is the control. Check it over while I get the photographs."

She had them in a folder and Bergman took it, spilling prints until he found the first taken after Enalus had stepped from the pod. He clipped it to the left-hand panel, adjusted the magnification, then placed another photograph he had brought with him into the right-hand section of the machine. A knurled knob twisted beneath his hand and, on a screen, both pictures appeared, one superimposed on the other, each in a different colour.

"You've set the machine wrong," said Nancy. "You've failed to adjust for scale-differential."

"No." Bergman flipped a switch and checked each of two ruby bands. "I made certain my photograph had a reference-scale. That table next to Enalus is exactly thirty-two inches in height. You used the normal scale-rod. Let's try again."

The pictures merged, the edges blurred a little and the woman sucked in her cheeks as she read the scales at the sides of the screen.

"She's grown, Professor. Hips are wider and breasts are larger and she seems a little taller than she did before."

"Two inches." Bergman was thoughtful. "And the increase is general, which makes the added height unnoticeable. The hair also tends to disguise the height and, naturally, her clothing acts as a distraction to her added bulk. Yet she is still in proportion."

And still very lovely—a goddess when compared to the human imperfections of the other women. Aphrodite must have looked like that, he thought, a vision of loveliness born from the foam to set a standard, an ideal that sculptors had tried for millennia to set in stone. A female so beautiful that, even in the trapped image of a photograph, she cast her enticing spell.

"Growing," said Nancy Coleman. "Professor, when did you take your photograph? Was it after Edward Markham died?"

"Yes, but there's no connection. There can't be; Enalus was cleared. She had a cast-iron alibi."

"One provided by a man," reminded the botanist. "Well, there's nothing we can do but wait. Edward could have been the victim of a freak accident or a rare natural condition, but if another man should die in similar circumstances, and if Enalus continues to grow—well, Professor, in that case the women will know what to do."

Koenig woke to the hum of his commlock, shedding dreams; nightmares in which he had run from faceless entities across an endless plain littered with bleached and ancient bones.

Helena looked from the screen. "There's something odd, John. You'd better come to Medical right away."

"Five minutes," he said. "No, make it ten."

He was dull with fatigue. There was no apparent emergency and a shower and cup of coffee would serve to restore his facilities. But why did he feel so tired?

In the shower he thought about it, reviewing the past few days. Markham's death had created a lot of work, alibis checked and rechecked, potential causes isolated and eliminated, a sea of faces to be questioned and tests and more tests to be made. All for no purpose. On the evidence nothing had caused the man's death but an unsuspected natural cause. An act of God, thought Koenig, the convenient blanket-cover used in the past to absolve everyone from blame. Too convenient—and Alpha could not afford the luxury of such self-indulgence.

"John?" Helena was calling again and with a start of guilt he realised that already the promised ten minutes had been doubled. He'd been dreaming in the shower, standing with his eyes closed, more asleep than awake. "John, are you well?"

"Yes." The question irritated him. "Why do you ask?"

"You look pale."

"I'm tired." He glanced at his watch. "Be with you in five minutes."

He made it with a minute to spare, looking around as he entered the Section, seeing the three men sitting like schoolboys on the long bench, the marks on their faces clear signals as to the violence in which they had participated.

"You called me here to see this?" Anger sharpened his voice. "Damn it, Helena, we have systems to handle such problems. Let Security take over—they know what to do."

"This isn't just a matter of discipline, John." The chill of her own voice was a reproof to his irritation. "And there is more than those three. George Tomlinson collapsed an hour ago."

"Dead?"

"No. We got to him in time. But he has the same symptoms as Constance Boswell had. The same illness that killed Edward Markham. John, he's been bled white!"

Koenig looked at the man as he lay in intensive care. The bluish light accentuated the corpse-like pallor of his face, the sunken cheeks and prominent bone adding to the appearance of a skull. A security guard was not chosen for his weakness, and Tomlinson, as Koenig remembered, had been a strong, sturdy, bull-like man with the smouldering strength of a horse.

"Anemia?"

"His blood is almost completely devoid of red corpuscles, John. But his collapse wasn't as sudden as Markham's. I've learned from his colleagues that for the past few days he's looked tired and jaded. They even made jokes about it—need I tell you what they were?"

"No." Koenig was aware of what they would have been. Aware, too, of the sudden anger that gripped him, the wave of emotion that dewed his face with sweat. "The swine!"

"John!"

"Nothing." He turned from the startled expression in her eyes. "What of the others? Those men out there? What made them fight?"

"Jealousy." Helena elaborated as she turned from the limp figure on the couch. "Something was said, someone objected and abruptly they were trying to kill each other. And I mean that literally, John. There are witnesses who will swear to it."

"Women?"

"Yes, but does it matter?" She didn't wait for an answer. "They were parted just in time and brought here. I've tranquillised them and made certain tests. John, they, too, are suffering from a shortage of red blood cells. They, too, are showing signs of anemia."

A plague? The very thought was terrifying, a gibbering nightmare that lurked forever at the threshold of awareness, a thing of white and ancient bone—one of the Four Horsemen that had always threatened man. And here, on the Moon, it was all the more horrible, for they had nowhere to run.

He said thickly, "What are you saying, Helena? A virus infection? A contaminating type of cancer? A mutated bacteria—for God's sake, woman! Tell me! Is Alpha doomed?"

"Steady!" He saw her face, the wide, startled eyes, the sudden expression of awareness replacing the previous concern. "You said you were tired, John, and you look paler than normal. Hold still a moment."

Her hand lifted and he felt the pressure of her fingers as she pulled down his lower eyelids. "I want to make a test, a blood count. It won't take long."

"Later. I'm—"

"Now, John!" Her tone precluded the concept of refusal, her authority paramount in such a case at such a time. "I must find out if you, too, have been affected."

"By what?"

"By the thing that has come among us," she said, bleakly. "The thing that is draining our blood."

CHAPTER THIRTEEN

There should have been wolves, creatures howling in a windswept darkness together with mouldering turrets and ancient castles with mysterious servants and an enigmatic nobleman who woke at sunset to prowl until dawn. A thing of legend, born from the need to explain the death that came from the dying of the blood, the increasing pallor of the afflicted. But, if vampires had ever existed, surely they must have been left far behind.

Surely it wasn't possible for one to be even now at large in Moonbase Alpha?

A thing to ponder, to add to the rest, a mountain of worry and doubt which, for the moment, he could do nothing about. Koenig sighed and looked at the ceiling, the bottle hanging from its support, the container of red, red blood that was being fed into his veins.

Tests had shown him to be anemic, the loss of red corpuscles accounting for his lassitude and irritation, or so Helena had explained. But how had he contracted the condition? How?

From where he sat at the side of the bed, Bergman said, "Helena is conducting a check on all personnel to determine how many are affected. As yet all those showing signs of anemia are men."

"Which means?"

"Perhaps nothing, but it is a fact and must be accepted as such. Men only—oddly enough Nancy Coleman hinted at potential trouble. She also suggested that at least half of us here in Alpha would know how to handle it."

"The women?" Koenig struggled to sit upright, feeling a momentary nausea, a jerk at the connection to his arm. Redness showed beneath the tape holding the hollow needle in place. Stripping it free, he removed the needle and folded his arm, holding his clenched hand hard against his shouder. "What nonsense is this, Victor?"

"Nonsense?"

"Yes. Enalus had nothing to do with this. She couldn't!"

Bergman said dryly, "Did I say she had, John? But now that you mention it, there is an interesting correlation between her and those affected. Every man showing signs of anemia has been close to her in some way. Edward Markham was her security escort and so was George Tomlinson. Those men who fought—two engineers and a hydroponics man—had spent time with her. And there are others. Everyone, John—every male who has been close to her shows some signs of a diminished red blood count."

"Rubbish! What about me? I—" Koenig broke off, conscious of Bergman's expression. "What's the matter, Victor? Why are you looking at me like that?"

"I'm wondering what's happened to your memory, John. You were alone with her in her room, remember? When we decided she was to be allowed the run of the Moonbase. And you spoke with her a couple of times since."

"So?"

"What happened in her room, John?"

"Nothing." Koenig was adamant. "We spoke and she stood before me and . . . and . . . nothing."

Nothing but a vague memory of something wonderful. A touch, a kiss, perhaps? He couldn't remember.

"Nothing," he said again. "It's all a coincidence. And you're forgetting the evidence. Enalus couldn't have been responsible for Markham's death. He was fit and well when he left her, and she didn't leave her room. We have proof of that."

"Tomlinson's word."

"Proof."

"All right, then, John, proof. But why be so upset? If she is innocent, then Enalus has nothing to be afraid of."

"Innocent?" Koenig swung his legs over the edge of the bed and stood upright. Again his senses swam to a momentary nausea and he wondered what else had been fed into his blood. Sedatives, perhaps? Antibiotics? Glucose and saline together with extract of liver? "Innocent? Victor, you talk as if she were on trial."

Bergman said flatly, "She is."

"By whose authority?"

"Helena— "

"Dr Russell is in charge of nothing but the Medical Section. She has no right to arrange a trial without my knowledge, *any* kind of a trial. Where is she? What has been going on? How long have I been here? Damn you, man, answer!"

Koenig heard the echoes and realised he had been shouting. An orderly looked into the room, her face startled, leaving to make room for Mathias, who came directly towards the two men.

"Commander! This is ridiculous! Get back on that bed immediately!"

"Go to hell!"

"What?"

"You heard me. Where is Dr Russell?" Koenig snarled deep in his throat. "Where is she? Damn it, do I have to take this place apart to find her?"

"She's in Main Mission. Commander— "

Koenig was already on his way.

She stood before the Moonbase monitoring screens watching the light and colour on the panels, the depicted scenes showing the various areas and those within them. A group sat in rapt enjoyment of a trio playing a complex melody on instruments fashioned of laminated metals and crystal, taut plastics and delicate ceramics. In Eden couples wandered along the paths, halting to enjoy the music of the fountain, the crops now well-established all around. In a starlit chamber with a transparent roof, deep chairs and secluded alcoves formed a rendezvous for the romantic.

Scenes that flickered and changed around one that held steady.

"Helena— "

She said without turning, "You should be in bed, John."

"Safely out of the way while you pass your judgements?" His tone was bitter. "You disappoint me, Helena. I thought you were above the petty emotions of jealousy and envy, yet here you are engaged on a witch hunt. What harm has Enalus ever done to you?"

She turned to face him and he was shaken by the sudden fury blazing in her eyes.

"More than you can imagine, John. And don't make the mistake of thinking that I have no emotions. Or are you implying that I'm not a real woman at all? Not as real, for example, as the thing you grew in a garden. Is that it?"

Bergman said soothingly, "This is a test, John, nothing more. Helena?"

"This isn't a trial," she said. "I'm not a judge and I would never presume to be a jury. But there is something we must know. Paul is helping me to find out. Sandra?"

"No change in temperature or ionic levels, Doctor," she reported from her instruments. "No trace of energy transfer as yet."

"What are you looking for?" Koenig looked around Main Mission. Aside from Morrow, the personnel was as he expected, but a relief man sat at the main console. "Where's Paul?"

"Here." Helena gestured at the static screen. "With Enalus."

They were framed like lovers in the panel edged with metal and alive with glowing colour. From the speakers came the sound of breathing, the soft strum of a guitar, the small noises of weight shifting on the bed where they sat. Paul Morrow had his back against a wall, the guitar in his hands, the girl at his side and leaning very close.

"Paul," she murmured, "play again, Paul, and tell me how you learned to make such wonderful music." Her hand lifted to caress his fingers. "You are so strong, so wonderful."

Koenig snarled his rage.

He felt it rise within him, a hot, tormenting flood that tinged the picture with red and sent the blood to roar in his ears.

"No," he said. "No! Get them out of there! Enalus! You can't! Enalus!"

At his side Bergman said quietly, "Hypersensitivity, as we suspected, Helena. Is there nothing we can do?"

"No, Victor. This is one battle he must win alone."

A battle of logic against emotion, of self against responsibility. He had derided Helena for being jealous, and now that same emotion threatened to tear him apart, to ruin his mind and crush his soul. He had sneered at her envy and now he would have given the rest of his life to be sitting where Morrow sat, to have the girl beside him as close.

"Paul," she whispered again, "do you like me a little? Do you trust me? I am so helpless here. I have no friends. I need a friend, Paul. Will you be my friend?"

"How can she do that?" Sandra was watching. "Look what she's doing to him!"

Helena said sharply, "Watch your instruments. The levels?"

"Remain the same, but— "

"She isn't human, Sandra. Remember that. She isn't human!"

And, perhaps, the more appealing because of it. An ideal holds more attraction than reality. The comfort of an illusion is not quickly thrown away. And no man, attacked at his basic, primeval, survival-structure, could resist the triggers of his biological drive.

"Enalus—you are beautiful! Enalus!"

She moved closer towards him, the mane of her hair falling over his face, shielding them both from the watching electronic eye. His hands fell from the guitar, one circling her waist, the other coming up to rest on her shoulder.

"Personal contact," whispered Bergman. "As I suspected. It would have to be something like that."

A touch. A kiss—why couldn't he remember?

Koenig drew in a deep breath, conscious of a battle won, of emotional turmoil stilled. Burned out, perhaps, a demon exorcised.

Sandra said quickly, "Doctor! The levels—"

"Sound the alarm. Have security move in. Quickly, girl! Quickly!"

On the screen Paul rolled from the enfolding embrace, his eyes glazed, his skin deathly pale.

Bergman said, "Well, there it is. Enalus is the cause of the anemia. The episode with Paul proves that beyond question. The amazing thing is that, even now, he insists that she didn't even touch him."

"A defence mechanism," said Helena. "I suspected it from the first. Any newly born creature must try to ensure protection against the environment. Enalus, from the first, emitted either a chemical or an electronic cloud of particles that caused a reaction in every male coming close to her." She added dryly, "I don't think I need to elaborate just what those reactions were."

Love, pity, compassion, jealousy—Koenig had felt

them all. The love that had gripped him in the Medical Section when first seeing the creature, the response to her plight when, later in her room, he had been overwhelmed with pity, an emotion perhaps even stronger than love.

"No one affected could endanger her in any way," mused Bergman. "Tomlinson lied, of course. She must have left her room to visit Markham, and he knew it, just as Paul lied in an attempt to protect her. As all the men with whom she came into contact lied as to the extent of their relationship. As they will continue to lie. They can't help it."

As he couldn't help his anger, thought Koenig. The rage that had turned his responsibility into nothing against the need to protect the girl. As he still felt the need to protect her.

"She's dangerous," said Helena, as if reading his thoughts. "An alien creature who has no conception of anything other than the need to survive. You must remember that at all times, John—you and everyone else in Alpha."

"You seem good at remembering, Helena."

"But I'm not the commander, John. I can't order that thing to be destroyed. You can."

"No! I— "

"You must," she insisted grimly. "One man is dead already because of her. It could have been two if we hadn't reached Tomlinson in time. More have lost blood to that . . . vampire. Are you going to risk the Moonbase for the sake of a delusion?"

"Helena, you're being unfair." Bergman looked at her from where he sat at the desk in Koenig's office. "You must remember that John has been exposed to the creature's defence-mechanism. He has been conditioned to protect her at any cost, and he isn't alone. There are others who will fight to the death to prevent you from hurting Enalus."

"If the men won't destroy her, then the women will," snapped Helena. "They won't be affected by the thing's defensive mechanisms."

"Perhaps not," admitted Bergman. "And I know from Nancy Coleman that you won't go short of volunteers. But suppose the men stand before her—will your women kill them in order to get at Enalus? And will the men permit the women to come close, knowing what they intend?"

"Civil war," said Helena bleakly, "and of the worst possible kind. Men against women, and neither side can hope to win—not unless they are willing to destroy the Moonbase. Damn you, Victor. What can we do?"

"Think." He leaned back, face graven with thought, looking detached and a little remote as he steepled his fingers. "Consider alternatives and try to be compassionate. Enalus is, first and foremost, only trying to survive. That is the prime objective of any organism. She seems to need blood in order to achieve that end. Now, is there any substitute she would accept instead? How much blood is essential to maintain her existence? Can we afford it? Could we reach some kind of a compromise? Is there any way in which—"

Koenig leaned back, barely listening to the flow of words, knowing they were only dressing to cover the real problem. Not an impasse, as had been suggested, but an outright confrontation.

And what if Enalus decided to take over Alpha?

The hum of his commlock broke an ugly train of thought and Koenig glared at the screen. The operator was quick to apologise.

"I'm sorry, Commander. I know you are in conference, but it's Dr Mathias. He says it is urgent."

"Very well." At least the interruption would provide a momentary relief from trying to solve the insoluble. "Put him on the communications post."

The screen flared to life and Mathias looked at the assembly.

"Commander! Professor! Dr Russell! I've discovered something that could be important. It has to do with the blood of the anemia victims."

"The blood?"

"Yes, Doctor. We have both been concerned at the absence of a visible wound that precludes the actual removal of blood from the body as would be the case in true vampirism. And when we checked we counted only the red corpuscles, correct? Well, I got to thinking and did a total count of all cells, both red and white. There was a shortage of red, right enough, but not a noticeable diminution in the total. What appears to have happened is that the red cells somehow lost their pigment."

"Their pigment! But how?" Bergman blinked, then said, "Of course! The haemoglobin! Helena, that means— "

"It means that Enalus didn't want blood at all," she said. "She wanted the iron it contained. The haemoglobin. Remove it and you produce anemia. John, don't you see, she wanted the iron!"

CHAPTER FOURTEEN

It was hard now to look at the screen—to see the image it displayed, the figure held fast in the room, one that had once held so much loveliness, so much grace. The change had been too sudden, thought Koenig, too great. And yet something still remained —the hair, long, fine, a shimmering waterfall that clothed the shoulders, the upper torso, the face. The emitted particles that still affected all who came physically close, making slaves of every male aside from Bergman, who seemed, in some remote fashion, to be immune.

Or, if not immune, then less affected than the others. As he was less affected now that he saw her only on a screen.

"John, has she fed yet?" Helena joined him where he stood at the monitor. She was tense, nerve and sinew keyed as if she were an engineer defusing a bomb. A good analogy, perhaps, but she could never be certain if she was defusing or triggering a device that could destroy them all. "Has Victor given her the ration?"

"He's doing it now."

Koenig watched as Bergman entered the room, female security guards passing him through, women wearing complete space armour, armed, under strict orders to shoot if Enalus should attempt to leave her quarters. He carried a large container in his hands. It held an allotropic form of iron, one devised and produced by Helena, a chemically accurate substitute for that carried in the blood and which gave the red cells their colour.

"Enalus?" He set it on a low table. "How do you feel?"

"I am well, Victor." The music of the voice remained, the initial mental contact long augmented by vocal communication, another facet of the defence mechanism. When had it happened, Koenig wondered. After I had accused her of using mental telepathy? Had she adapted, then, to conform? "You have brought me more iron?"

She lifted the container and turned so that her back was towards Bergman and the scanner of the monitor. Beneath the mane of her hair her shoulders moved a little as she lowered her face over the jar. Then she straightened and turned again and set it down empty.

"More, Victor. I must have more."

"You will get it," he promised. "Together with food. You still need food?"

"Yes. Food and water, but, most of all, iron. I need it as you need salt. You understand, Victor? To me it is life."

A life that had hung in the balance. Koenig remembered the discussions, the savage intensity that had almost turned into physical violence. The discovery of her need for iron had given them a weapon against her. It was a revealed weakness that had altered the entire situation. Now there had been no need to take violent action against her. All they need do was to refuse her access to the essential element.

"She will die," said Helena. "Deprived of it, she will cease to exist. John, we are safe!"

"At the cost of what?" Bergman had glared his

frustration. "A new form of life, Helena, and you want to destroy it. Are we barbarians? Have we no mercy, no tolerance? Must we kill simply because we cannot understand?"

"She is alien."

"She deserves a chance."

"She should be eliminated."

"She could teach us things we don't even suspect exist." Bergman appealed to Koenig. "John, we can't waste this opportunity. We had to destroy the parasite, that I agree, but not Enalus. She—please, John, not Enalus."

They had watched him, one wanting him to decide to destroy, the other for him to be merciful. For a moment he had hesitated and then—had Enalus herself guided his decision?—had said, "There is no need to be hasty. Let us hold her safe, feed her the iron and see what happens. You agree, Victor?"

"Yes, John. Of course!"

"Helena?"

"You are the commander, John. I hope you don't regret it."

A wish she repeated as they now stood together facing the screen.

"She was so lovely and now—John, would it have been better to have let her die?"

"No."

"But look at her. As a woman I can understand what she must be feeling. If I were in her place—"

She broke off as he took her by the shoulders and turned her to face him. "You're not, Helena. And don't make the same mistake you've warned me against so often. Enalus isn't a woman. She is an alien creature. She isn't human, Helena."

It was his turn to give her strength, to bolster her clinical detachment and to point out the absence of need of a woman's pity. Yet it was hard for Helena not to feel compassion. Hard for anyone who had known Enalus not to compare what she had been with what she had become.

On the screen she moved again, slowly, turning like a billowing sail in the wind, huge, rounded, shapeless. A swollen travesty of the lithe young girl she had once seemed.

Watching her, Koenig felt a yearning regret.

"Metamorphosis," said Bergman. "It has to be. It's the only thing that explains all the facts as we know them. Enalus is on the verge of undergoing change."

"Helena?"

"Victor is right, John." She glanced at her notes. "And it will be soon. Her size has remained static for the past two days and she has ceased all ingestion of all food and liquids, including the iron. She seems now to be dormant, and no movement has been observed for the past three hours."

"But metamorphosis?" Koenig moved impatiently about his office. "She came from a plant, remember? How can a fruit change its shape?"

"On Earth it can't," admitted Bergman. "I've spoken to Nancy about it and she is positive. But we are dealing with an alien form of life, John, and one that must follow alien rules. And even on Earth there are some pretty exotic forms of life-cycle. Think of bees, for example. The grubs are the same, but when sealed into their cells, they are fed differently and the diet determines the shape they will adopt as adults: some are workers; some are drones; others are queens. Termites have an even greater variation."

Small insects and easily handled, but Koenig remembered the thing that had ridden in the pod from space and how close it had come to destroying the Moonbase. A risk he had no intention of running again.

He said flatly, "You want the change to take place, right?" Then, as Bergman nodded he added, "You realise the risk. Victor? We have no way of telling what may emerge after the transformation is complete. Enalus had strong defence mechanisms and she was, according to your theory, only an unsophisticated form of life. Have you imagined what the next stage could be?"

Helena said quietly, "You want to destroy her, John?"

They could do it now if they wanted to, and perhaps it was the only chance they would get. The creature was bloated, dormant, helpless. Lasers could sear it to ash, cut it into segments, burn and char whatever lay beneath the human-like skin. To kill now would be easy. To destroy would be safe.

Koenig looked down at his hands. They were clenched, the nails biting into his palms, the knuckles white. To kill! To destroy! To eliminate the unknown and the fear that accompanied it!

Within the deepest recesses of his mind a primitive, ape-like thing lifted its head to howl at the Moon.

"Helena?"

"At the moment Enalus is harmless. I must admit to a certain curiosity as to what shape she may adopt, and there is medical knowledge to be gained by forbearance, but—" She let her voice trail into silence.

A silence broken by Bergman.

"John, she must be given her chance. It is a gamble, I admit, but one we have taken before. We gave her the iron, and so we helped her to the next stage of her development. Are we now to change our minds? And think a little of the nature she has already displayed."

"I am," said Koenig bleakly. "One man dead and another placed at risk."

"Accidents, John. She had no way of knowing the danger level of diminished haemoglobin. She was driven to absorb the essential element and Markham provided the iron. She took too much and almost made the same error later with Tomlinson. But she didn't make it, John. And later she controlled her demands. Helena, were any of the other victims seriously at risk?"

"No," she admitted. "Given time, all would have recovered without aid."

"So she was merciful—was that the act of a savage? Since we gave her iron, has she attempted to take it from any other source? She has been confined, I know, but I've been with her and so has Helena and other women. None have been touched."

"So you want her to be left alone?"

"Yes."

For the sake of the knowledge she . . . it . . . could give. The old, old curse of the scientists who, in ancient days, would cheerfully have made a pact with the devil for the sake of opening doors to new vistas of attainment. How many had died breathing the noxious fumes rising from their alembics? How many had poisoned themselves with the use of strange chemicals, gases, compounds? Men armed only with ignorance and the determination to know. To learn. To understand.

Could he do less?

Later, standing before the transparent partition separating him and the others from Enalus where she lay on her couch, he pondered the question, adding another.

Had he the justification to learn at the expense of others? Was the risk to Alpha too great? Did any man have the right to gain knowledge when the price was misery and unhappiness to the majority?

Questions there was no time to answer. Helena caught his arm, the sound of her indrawn breath loud in the strained silence. "John! She's moving!"

A twitch, no more, and one over as soon as it had begun. Beyond the walls guards stood ready with weapons at hand. In Main Mission electronic scanners watched every move and monitored all energy levels, recording and correlating even as they observed. Here, with no possibility of electronic distortion, Koenig waited for a biological miracle.

The transformation of living flesh and tissue from one form to another.

But, no, not flesh, from plant into—what?

"John!"

He strained forward as Helena squeezed his arm. Beyond the partition the slumped figure stirred again, seemed to turn, to writhe, to split.

To turn into a blazing scintillation of lambent, coruscating, eye-bright glory.

It was something he had never experienced before and even as he slumped to sprawl on the floor, eyes tightly closed, hands lifted to protect the lids, a part of Koenig's mind tried to fit the explicable to the inexplicable. Matter converted into energy, light used as a non-material halo, different energy levels that registered on limited senses in crude analogies.

And a presence that filled his brain with awe.

"You were kind, and for that I thank you. Such impulses do you credit. Already you are high on the ladder that leads to the ultimate. Imagination and compassion—these are the keys to true humanity."

"You—Enalus?"

"I." The voice echoed in the recesses of his mind, communication without the need of hampering words, ideas and concepts relayed in their entirety without distortion. "You knew me best when I was younger, and then I did things that I could not avoid. But to forgive was to show understanding. And now for me one journey is over."

"But how?"

A blur of thoughts, a seed, a plant, an aching void, the tenderness of remembered affection, the pang of recalled jealousy. A montage of emotions and questions that flooded his mind and which, before his mental apparatus could sort and assemble them in any order, had already been understood.

And answered.

A life-cycle of staggering complexity; from a spore to an insect to a bird, a fish, a plant, the girl-shape he had known to—an angel?

A long, long path to a higher evolution, attended by incredible risk each step of the way, luck and circumstance alone deciding success.

Was it possible?

On Earth there were life-forms that defied extinction; flukes that needed an intermediate host; oysters that spawned billions of eggs in order that a few should survive; humanity itself, which operated on the same level of multiple seed-production."

How many men had failed to survive beyond the womb?

How many had succumbed before achieving their full potential?

Yes, it was possible, and more than possible.

"You are wise. Small and helpless as you are, yet in you there is great wisdom. Now I must leave to join those who have gone before. But remember always, shape and form are only the result of environment and chance—but love and compassion are universal. Farewell!"

Light pulsed around them with a tangible pressure and then, suddenly, was gone. Weakly, Koenig climbed to his feet. The chamber beyond the partition was empty. For a brief moment it had held a higher order of life that had passed through the walls and roof as if they did not exist. A form of life that even now was hurtling across space to the place where it belonged.

And Alpha was his again.